THE
LATHE
OF
HEAVEN

URSULA K. LE GUIN

THE LATHE OF HEAVEN

AVON
PUBLISHERS OF BARD, CAMELOT, DISCUS, EQUINOX AND FLARE BOOKS

First published in Amazing Stories Magazine.

Portions of the lyrics to the song, "With a Little Help From My Friends" (Lennon-McCartney) (Copyright © 1967 by Northern Sons Limited) are used by permission of Maclen Music, Inc. All rights reserved.

AVON BOOKS
A division of
The Hearst Corporation
959 Eighth Avenue
New York, New York 10019

First Avon Printing, April, 1973.

Printed in the U.S.A.

THE
LATHE
OF
HEAVEN

1

Confucius and you are both dreams, and I who
say you are dreams am a dream myself. This is a
paradox. Tomorrow a wise man may explain it;
that tomorrow will not be for ten thousand gen-
erations.

—Chuang Tse: II

Current-borne, wave-flung, tugged hugely by the whole
might of ocean, the jellyfish drifts in the tidal abyss. The
light shines through it, and the dark enters it. Borne, flung,
tugged from anywhere to anywhere, for in the deep sea
there is no compass but nearer and farther, higher and
lower, the jellyfish hangs and sways; pulses move slight and
quick within it, as the vast diurnal pulses beat in the
moondriven sea. Hanging, swaying, pulsing, the most
vulnerable and insubstantial creature, it has for its defense
the violence and power of the whole ocean, to which it has
entrusted its being, its going, and its will.

But here rise the stubborn continents. The shelves of
gravel and the cliffs of rock break from water baldly into
air, that dry, terrible outerspace of radiance and instability,
where there is no support for life. And now, now the
currents mislead and the waves betray, breaking their
endless circle, to leap up in loud foam against rock and
air, breaking. . . .

What will the creature made all of seadrift do on the dry
sand of daylight; what will the mind do, each morning,
waking?

His eyelids had been burned away, so that he could not
close his eyes, and the light entered into his brain, searing.

He could not turn his head, for blocks of fallen concrete pinned him down and the steel rods projecting from their cores held his head in a vise. When these were gone he could move again; he sat up. He was on the cement steps; a dandelion flowered by his hand, growing from a little cracked place in the steps. After a while he stood up, but as soon as he was on his feet he felt deathly sick, and knew it was the radiation sickness. The door was only two feet from him, for the balloonbed when inflated half filled his room. He got to the door and opened it and went through it. There stretched the endless linoleum corridor, heaving slightly up and down for miles, and far down it, very far, the men's room. He started out toward it, trying to hold on to the wall, but there was nothing to hold on to, and the wall turned into the floor.

"Easy now. Easy there."

The elevator guard's face was hanging above him like a paper lantern, pallid, fringed with graying hair.

"It's the radiation," he said, but Mannie didn't seem to understand, saying only, "Take it easy."

He was back on his bed in his room.

"You drunk?"

"No."

"High on something?"

"Sick."

"What you been taking?"

"Couldn't find the fit," he said, meaning that he had been trying to lock the door through which the dreams came, but none of the keys had fit the lock.

"Medic's coming up from the fifteenth floor," Mannie said faintly through the roar of breaking seas.

He was floundering and trying to breathe. A stranger was sitting on his bed holding a hypodermic and looking at him.

"That did it," the stranger said. "He's coming round. Feel like hell? Take it easy. You ought to feel like hell. Take all this at once?" He displayed seven of the little plastifoil envelopes from the autodrug dispensary. "Lousy mixture, barbiturates and Dexedrine. What were you trying to do to yourself?"

8

It was hard to breathe, but the sickness was gone, leaving only an awful weakness.

"They're all dated this week," the medic went on, a young man with a brown ponytail and bad teeth. "Which means they're not all off your own Pharmacy Card, so I've got to report you for borrowing. I don't like to, but I got called in and I haven't any choice, see. But don't worry, with these drugs it's not a felony, you'll just get a notice to report to the police station and they'll send you up to the Med School or the Area Clinic for examination, and you'll be referred to an M.D. or a shrink for VTT—Voluntary Therapeutic Treatment. I filled out the form on you already, used your ID; all I need to know is how long you been using these drugs in more than your personal allotment?"

"Couple months."

The medic scribbled on a paper on his knee.

"And who'd you borrow Pharm Cards from?"

"Friends."

"Got to have the names."

After a while the medic said, "One name, anyhow. Just a formality. It won't get 'em in trouble. See, they'll just get a reprimand from the police, and HEW Control will keep a check on their Pharm Cards for a year. Just a formality. One name."

"I can't. They were trying to help me."

"Look, if you won't give the names, you're resisting, and you'll either go to jail or get stuck into Obligatory Therapy, in an institution. Anyway they can trace the cards through the autodrug records if they want to, this just saves 'em time. Come on, just give me one of the names."

He covered his face with his arms to keep out the unendurable light and said, "I can't. I can't do it. I need help."

"He borrowed my card," the elevator guard said. "Yeah. Mannie Ahrens, 247-602-6023." The medic's pen went scribble scribble.

"I never used your card."

"So confuse 'em a little. They won't check. People use

people's Pharm Cards all the time, they can't check. I loan mine, use another cat's, all the time. Got a whole collection of those reprimand things. They don't know. I taken things HEW never even *heard* of. You ain't been on the hook before. Take it easy, George."

"I can't," he said, meaning that he could not let Mannie lie for him, could not stop him from lying for him, could not take it easy, could not go on.

"You'll feel better in two, three hours," the medic said. "But stay in today. Anyhow downtown's all tied up, the GPRT drivers are trying another strike and the National Guard's trying to run the subway trains and the news says it's one hell of a mess. Stay put. I got to go, I walk to work, damn it, ten minutes from here, that State Housing Complex down on Macadam." The bed jounced as he stood up. "You know there's two hundred sixty kids in that one complex suffering from kwashiorkor? All low-income or Basic Support families, and they aren't getting protein. And what the hell am I supposed to do about it? I've put in five different reqs for Minimal Protein Ration for those kids and they don't come, it's all red tape and excuses. People on Basic Support can afford to buy sufficient food, they keep telling me. Sure, but what if the food isn't there to buy? Ah, the hell with it. I go give 'em Vitamin C shots and try to pretend that starvation is just scurvy. . . ."

The door shut. The bed jounced when Mannie sat down on it where the medic had been sitting. There was a faint smell, sweetish, like newly cut grass. Out of the darkness of closed eyes, the mist rising all round, Mannie's voice said remotely, "Ain't it great to be alive?"

2

The portal of God is non-existence.
—Chuang Tse: XXIII

Dr. William Haber's office did not have a view of Mount Hood. It was an interior Efficiency Suite on the sixty-third floor of Willamette East Tower and didn't have a view of anything. But on one of the windowless walls was a big photographic mural of Mount Hood, and at this Dr. Haber gazed while intercommunicating with his receptionist.

"Who's this Orr coming up, Penny? The hysteric with leprosy symptoms?"

She was only three feet away through the wall, but an interoffice communicator, like a diploma on the wall, inspires confidence in the patient, as well as in the doctor. And it is not seemly for a psychiatrist to open the door and shout, "Next!"

"No, Doctor, that's Mr. Greene tomorrow at ten. This is the referral from Dr. Walters at the University Medical School, a VTT case."

"Drug abuse. Right. Got the file here. O.K., send him in when he comes."

Even as he spoke he could hear the elevator whine up and stop, the doors gasp open; then footsteps, hesitation, the outer door opening. He could also, now he was listening, hear doors, typewriters, voices, toilets flushing, in offices all up and down the hall and above him and underneath him. The real trick was to learn how not to hear them. The only solid partitions left were inside the head.

Now Penny was going through the first-visit routine

11

with the patient, and while waiting Dr. Haber gazed again at the mural and wondered when such a photograph had been taken. Blue sky, snow from foothills to peak. Years ago, in the sixties or seventies, no doubt. The Greenhouse Effect had been quite gradual, and Haber, born in 1962, could clearly remember the blue skies of his childhood. Nowadays the eternal snows were gone from all the world's mountains, even Everest, even Erebus, fiery-throated on the waste Antarctic shore. But of course they might have colored a modern photograph, faked the blue sky and white peak; no telling.

"Good afternoon, Mr. Orr!" he said, rising, smiling, but not extending his hands, for many patients these days had a strong dread of physical contact.

The patient uncertainly withdrew his almost-proffered hand, fingered his necklace nervously, and said, "How do you do." The necklace was the usual long chain of silvered steel. Clothing ordinary, office-worker standard; haircut conservative shoulder-length, beard short. Light hair and eyes, a short, slight, fair man, slightly undernourished, good health, 28 to 32. Unaggressive, placid, milquetoast, repressed, conventional. The most valuable period of relationship with a patient, Haber often said, is the first ten seconds.

"Sit down, Mr. Orr. Right! Do you smoke? The brown filters are tranks, the white are denicks." Orr did not smoke. "Now, let's see if we're together on your situation. HEW Control wants to know why you've been borrowing your friends' Pharmacy Cards to get more than your allotment of pep pills and sleeping pills from the autodrug. Right? So they sent you up to the boys on the hill, and they recommended Voluntary Therapeutic Treatment and sent you over to me for the therapy. All correct?"

He heard his own genial, easy tone, well calculated to put the other person at his ease; but this one was still far from easy. He blinked often, his sitting posture was tense, the position of his hands was overformal: a classic picture of suppressed anxiety. He nodded as if he was gulping at the same moment.

"O.K., fine, nothing out of the way there. If you'd been

stockpiling your pills, to sell to addicts or commit a murder with, then you'd be in hot water. But as you simply used 'em, your punishment's no worse than a few sessions with me! Now of course what I want to know is *why* you used 'em, so that together we can work out some better life pattern for you, that'll keep you within the dosage limits of your own Pharm Card for one thing, and perhaps for another set you free of any drug dependency at all. Now your routine," his eyes went for a moment to the folder sent down from the Med School, "was to take barbiturates for a couple of weeks, then switch for a few nights to dextroamphetamine, then back to the barbiturates. How did that get started? Insomnia?"

"I sleep well."

"But you have bad dreams."

The man looked up, frightened: a flash of open terror. He was going to be a simple case. He had no defenses.

"Sort of," he said huskily.

"It was an easy guess for me, Mr. Orr. They generally send me the dreamers." He grinned at the little man. "I'm a dream specialist. Literally. An oneirologist. Sleep and dreaming are my field. O.K., now I can proceed to the next educated guess, which is that you used the phenobarb to suppress dreaming but found that with habituation the drug has less and less dream-suppressive effect, until it has none at all. Similarly with the Dexedrine. So you alternated them. Right?"

The patient nodded stiffly.

"Why was your stretch on the Dexedrine always shorter?"

"It made me jumpy."

"I'll bet it did. And that last combination dose you took was a lulu. But not, in itself, dangerous. All the same, Mr. Orr, you were doing something dangerous." He paused for effect. "You were depriving yourself of dreams."

Again the patient nodded.

"Do you try to deprive yourself of food and water, Mr. Orr? Have you tried doing without air lately?"

He kept his tone jovial, and the patient managed a brief unhappy smile.

13

"You know that you need sleep. Just as you need food, water, and air. But did you realize that sleep's not enough, that your body insists just as strongly upon having its allotment of *dreaming* sleep? If deprived systematically of dreams, your brain will do some very odd things to you. It will make you irritable, hungry, unable to concentrate— does this sound familiar? It wasn't just the Dexedrine!— liable to daydreams, uneven as to reaction times, forgetful, irresponsible, and prone to paranoid fantasies. And finally it will force you to dream—no matter what. No drug we have will keep you from dreaming, unless it kills you. For instance, extreme alcoholism can lead to a condition called central pontine myelinolysis, which is fatal; its cause is a lesion in the lower brain resulting from lack of dreaming. Not from lack of sleep! From lack of the very specific state that occurs during sleep, the dreaming state, REM sleep, the d-state. Now you're no alcoholic, and not dead, and so I know that whatever you've taken to suppress your dreams, it's worked only partially. Therefore, (a) you're in poor shape physically from partial dream deprivation, and (b) you've been trying to go up a blind alley. Now. What started you up the blind alley? A fear of dreams, of bad dreams, I take it, or what you consider to be bad dreams. Can you tell me anything about these dreams?"

Orr hesitated.

Haber opened his mouth and shut it again. So often he knew what his patients were going to say, and could say it for them better than they could say it for themselves. But it was their taking the step that counted. He could not take it for them. And after all, this talking was a mere preliminary, a vestigial rite from the palmy days of analysis; its only function was to help him decide how he should help the patient, whether positive or negative conditioning was indicated, what he should *do*.

"I don't have nightmares more than most people, I think," Orr was saying, looking down at his hands. "Nothing special. I'm . . . afraid of dreaming."

"Of dreaming bad dreams."

"Any dreams."

"I see. Have you any notion how that fear got started? Or what it is you're afraid of, wish to avoid?"

As Orr did not reply at once, but sat looking down at his hands, square, reddish hands lying too still on his knee, Haber prompted just a little. "Is it the irrationality, the lawlessness, sometimes the immorality of dreams, is it something like that that makes you uncomfortable?"

"Yes, in a way. But for a specific reason. You see, here . . . here I . . ."

Here's the crux, the lock, though Haber, also watching those tense hands. Poor bastard. He has wet dreams, and a guilt complex about 'em. Boyhood enuresis, compulsive mother—

"Here's where you stop believing me."

The little fellow was sicker than he looked.

"A man who deals with dreams both awake and sleeping isn't too concerned with belief and disbelief, Mr. Orr. They're not categories I use much. They don't apply. So ignore that, and go on. I'm interested." Did that sound patronizing? He looked at Orr to see if the statement had been taken amiss, and met, for one instant, the man's eyes. Extraordinarily beautiful eyes, Haber thought, and was surprised by the word, for beauty was not a category he used much either. The irises were blue or gray, very clear, as if transparent. For a moment Haber forgot himself and stared back at those clear, elusive eyes; but only for a moment, so that the strangeness of the experience scarcely registered on his conscious mind.

"Well," Orr said, speaking with some determination, "I have had dreams that . . . that affected the . . . non-dream world. The real world."

"We all have, Mr. Orr."

Orr stared. The perfect straight man.

"The effect of the dreams of the just prewaking d-state on the general emotional level of the psyche can be—"

But the straight man interrupted him. "No, I don't mean that." And stuttering a little, "What I mean is, I dreamed something, and it came true."

"That isn't hard to believe, Mr. Orr. I'm quite serious in saying that. It's only since the rise of scientific thought

15

that anybody much has been inclined even to question such a statement, much less disbelieve it. Prophetic—"

"Not prophetic dreams. I can't foresee anything. I simply *change* things." The hands were clenched tight. No wonder the Med School bigwigs had sent this one here. They always sent the nuts they couldn't crack to Haber.

"Can you give me an example? For instance, can you recall the very first time that you had such a dream? How old were you?"

The patient hesitated a long time, and finally said, "Sixteen, I think." His manner was still docile; he showed considerable fear of the subject, but no defensiveness or hostility toward Haber. "I'm not sure."

"Tell me about the first time you're sure of."

"I was seventeen. I was still living at home, and my mother's sister was staying with us. She was getting a divorce and wasn't working, just getting Basic Support. She was kind of in the way. It was a regular three-room flat, and she was always there. Drove my mother up the wall. She wasn't considerate, Aunt Ethel, I mean. Hogged the bathroom—we still had a private bathroom in that flat. And she kept, oh, making a sort of joking play for me. Half joking. Coming into my bedroom in her topless pajamas, and so on. She was only about thirty. It got me kind of uptight. I didn't have a girl yet and . . . you know. Adolescents. It's easy to get a kid worked up. I resented it. I mean, she was my aunt."

He glanced at Haber to make sure that the doctor knew what he had resented, and did not disapprove of his resentment. The insistent permissiveness of the late Twentieth Century had produced fully as much sex-guilt and sex-fear in its heirs as had the insistent repressiveness of the late Nineteenth Century. Orr was afraid that Haber might be shocked at his not wanting to go to bed with his aunt. Haber maintained his noncommittal but interested expression, and Orr plowed on.

"Well, I had a lot of sort of anxiety dreams, and this aunt was always in them. Usually disguised, the way people are in dreams sometimes; once she was a white cat, but I knew she was Ethel, too. Anyhow, finally one night when she'd got me to take her to the movies, and tried to get me to handle her, and then when we got home she kept flopping around on my bed and saying how my parents were asleep and so on, well, after I finally got her out of my room and got to sleep, I had this dream. A very vivid one. I could recall it completely when I woke up. I dreamed that Ethel had been killed in a car crash in Los Angeles, and the telegram had come. My mother was crying while she was trying to cook dinner, and I felt sorry for her, and kept wishing I could do something for her, but I didn't know what to do. That was all. . . . Only when I got up, I went into the living room. No Ethel on the couch. There wasn't anybody else in the apartment, just my parents and me. She wasn't there. She never had been there. I didn't have to ask. I remembered. I knew that Aunt Ethel had been killed in a crash on a Los Angeles freeway six weeks ago, coming home after seeing a lawyer about getting a divorce. We had got the news by telegram. The whole dream was just sort of reliving something like what had actually happened. Only it hadn't happened. Until the dream. I mean, I *also* knew that she'd been living with us, sleeping on the couch in the living room, until last night."

"But there was nothing to show that, to prove it?"

"No. Nothing. She hadn't been. Nobody remembered that she had been, except me. And I was wrong. Now."

Haber nodded judiciously and stroked his beard. What had seemed a mild drug-habituation case now appeared to be a severe aberration, but he had never had a delusion system presented to him quite so straightforwardly. Orr might be an intelligent schizophrenic, feeding him a line, putting him on, with schizoid inventiveness and deviousness; but he lacked the faint inward arrogance of such people, to which Haber was extremely sensitive.

"Why do you think your mother didn't notice that reality had changed since last night?"

"Well, she didn't dream it. I mean, the dream really did change reality. It made a different reality, retroactively, which she'd been part of all along. Being in it, she had no memory of any other. I did, I remembered both, because I

17

was . . . there . . . at the moment of the change. This is the only way I can explain it, I know it doesn't make sense. But I have got to have some explanation, or else face the fact that I am insane."

No, this fellow was no milquetoast.

"I'm not in the judgment business, Mr. Orr. I'm after facts. And the events of the mind, believe me, to me are facts. When you *see* another man's dream as he dreams it recorded in black and white on the electroencephalograph, as I've done ten thousand times, you don't speak of dreams as 'unreal.' They exist; they are events; they leave a mark behind them. O.K. I take it that you had other dreams that seemed to have this same sort of effect?"

"Some. Not for a long time. Only under stress. But it seemed to . . . to be happening oftener. I began to get scared."

Haber leaned forward. "Why?"

Orr looked blank.

"Why scared?"

"Because I don't want to change things!" Orr said, as if stating the superobvious. "Who am I to meddle with the way things go? And it's my unconscious mind that changes things, without any intelligent control. I tried autohypnosis but it didn't do any good. Dreams are incoherent, selfish, irrational—immoral, you said a minute ago. They come from the unsocialized part of us, don't they, at least partly? I didn't want to kill poor Ethel. I just wanted her out of my way. Well, in a dream, that's likely to be drastic. Dreams take short cuts. I killed her. In a car crash a thousand miles away six weeks ago. I am responsible for her death."

Haber stroked his beard again. "Therefore," he said slowly, "the dream-suppressant drugs. So that you will avoid further responsibilities."

"Yes. The drugs kept the dreams from building up and getting vivid. It's only certain ones, very intense ones, that are. . . ." He sought a word, "effective."

"Right. O.K. Now, let's see. You're unmarried; you're a draftsman for the Bonneville-Umatilla Power District. How do you like your work?"

18

"Fine."

"How's your sex life?"

"Had one trial marriage. Broke up last summer, after a couple of years."

"Did you pull out, or she?"

"Both of us. She didn't want a kid. It wasn't full-marriage material."

"And since then?"

"Well, there're some girls at my office, I'm not a . . . not a great stud, actually."

"How about interpersonal relationships in general? Do you feel you relate satisfactorily to other people, that you have a niche in the emotional ecology of your environment?"

"I guess so."

"So that you could say that there's nothing really wrong with your life. Right? O.K. Now tell me this; do you want, do you seriously want, to get out of this drug dependency?"

"Yes."

"O.K., good. Now, you've been taking drugs because you want to keep from dreaming. But not all dreams are dangerous; only certain vivid ones. You dreamed of your Aunt Ethel as a white cat, but she wasn't a white cat next morning—right? Some dreams are all right—safe."

He waited for Orr's assenting nod.

"Now, think about this. How would you feel about testing this whole thing out, and perhaps learning how to dream safely, without fear? Let me explain. You've got the subject of dreaming pretty loaded emotionally. You are literally afraid to dream because you feel that some of your dreams have this capacity to affect real life, in ways you can't control. Now, that may be an elaborate and meaningful metaphor, by which your unconscious mind is trying to tell your conscious mind something about reality —your reality, your life—which you aren't ready, rationally, to accept. But we can take the metaphor quite literally; there's no need to translate it, at this point, into rational terms. Your problem at present is this: you're afraid to dream, and yet you need to dream. You tried suppression by drugs; it didn't work. O.K., let's try the opposite. Let's get you to dream, intentionally. Let's get you to dream, intensely and vividly, right here. Under my supervision, under controlled conditions. So that *you* can get control over what seems to you to have got out of hand."

"How can I dream to order?" Orr said with extreme discomfort.

"In Doctor Haber's Palace of Dreams, you can! Have you been hypnotized?"

"For dental work."

"Good. O.K. Here's the system. I put you into hypnotic trance and suggest that you're going to sleep, that you're going to dream, and *what* you're going to dream. You'll wear a trancap to ensure that you have genuine sleep, not just hypnotrance. While you're dreaming I watch you, physically and on the EEG, the whole time. I wake you, and we talk about the dream experience. If it's gone off safely, perhaps you'll feel a bit easier about facing the next dream."

"But I won't dream effectively here; it only happens in one dream out of dozens or hundreds." Orr's defensive rationalizations were quite consistent.

"You can dream any style dream at all here. Dream content and dream affect can be controlled almost totally by a motivated subject and a properly trained hypnotizer. I've been doing it for ten years. And you'll be right there with me, because you'll be wearing a trancap. Ever worn one?"

Orr shook his head.

"You know what they are, though."

"They send a signal through electrodes that stimulates the . . . the brain to go along with it."

"That's roughly it. The Russians have been using it for fifty years, the Israelis refined on it, we finally climbed aboard and mass-produced it for professional use in calming psychotic patients and for home use in inducing sleep or alpha trance. Now, I was working a couple of years ago with a severely depressed patient on OTT at Linnton. Like many depressives she didn't get much sleep and was particularly short of d-state sleep, dreaming-sleep; whenever she did enter the d-state she tended to wake up. Vicious-circle effect: more depression—less dreams; less dreams—more depression. Break it. How? No drug we have does much to increase d-sleep. ESB—electronic brain stimulation? But that involves implanting electrodes, and deep, for the sleep centers; rather avoid an operation. I was using the trancap on her to encourage sleep. What if you made the diffuse, low-frequency signal more specific, directed it locally to the specific area within the brain; oh yes, sure, Dr. Haber, that's a snap! But actually, once I got the requisite electronics research under my belt, it only took a couple of months to work out the basic machine. Then I tried stimulating the subject's brain with a recording of brain waves from a healthy subject in the appropriate states, the various stages of sleep and dreaming. Not much luck. Found a signal from another brain may or may not pick up a response in the subject; had to learn to generalize, to make a sort of average, out of hundreds of normal brain-wave records. Then, as I work with the patient, I narrow it down again, tailor it: whenever the subject's brain is doing what I want it to do more of, I record that moment, augment it, enlarge and prolong it, replay it, and stimulate the brain to go along with its own healthiest impulses, if you'll excuse the pun. Now all that involved an enormous amount of feedback analysis, so that a simple EEG-plus-trancap grew into this," and he gestured to the electronic forest behind Orr. He had hidden most of it behind plastic paneling, for many patients were either scared of machinery or overidentified with it, but still it took up about a quarter of the office. "That's the Dream Machine," he said with a grin, "or, prosaically, the Augmentor; and what it'll do for you is ensure that you do go to sleep and that you dream—as briefly and lightly, or as long and intensively, as we like. Oh, incidentally, the depressive patient was discharged from Linnton this last summer as fully cured." He leaned forward. "Willing to give it a try?"

"Now?"

"What do you want to wait for?"

"But I can't fall asleep at four-thirty in the afternoon—" Then he looked foolish. Haber had been digging in the overcrowded drawer of his desk, and now produced a paper, the Consent to Hypnosis form required by HEW. Orr took the pen Haber held out, signed the form, and put it submissively down on the desk.

"All right. Good. Now, tell me this, George. Does your dentist use a Hypnotape, or is he a do-it-yourself man?"

"Tape. I'm 3 on the susceptibility scale."

"Right in the middle of the graph, eh? Well, for suggestion as to dream content to work well, we'll want fairly deep trance. We don't want a trance dream, but a genuine sleep dream; the Augmentor will provide that; but we want to be sure the suggestion goes pretty deep. So, to avoid spending hours in just conditioning you to enter deep trance, we'll use v-c induction. Ever seen it done?"

Orr shook his head. He looked apprehensive, but he offered no objection. There was an acceptant, passive quality about him that seemed feminine, or even childish. Haber recognized in himself a protective/bullying reaction toward this physically slight and compliant man. To dominate, to patronize him was so easy as to be almost irresistible.

"I use it on most patients. It's fast, safe, and sure—by far the best method of inducing hypnosis, and the least trouble for both hypnotist and subject." Orr would certainly have heard the scare stories about subjects being brain-damaged or killed by overprolonged or inept v-c induction, and though such fears did not apply here, Haber must pander to them and calm them, lest Orr resist the whole induction. So he went on with the patter, describing the fifty-year history of the v-c induction method and then veering off the subject of hypnosis altogether, back to the subject of sleep and dreams, in order to get Orr's attention off the induction process and on to the aim of it. "The gap we have to bridge, you see, is the gulf that exists between the waking or hypnotized-trance condition and the dreaming state. That gulf has a common name: sleep. Normal sleep, the s-state, non-REM sleep, whichever name you like. Now, there are, roughly speaking, four mental states

22

with which we're concerned: waking, trance, s-sleep, and d-state. If you look at mentation processes, the s-state, the d-state, and the hypnotic state all have something in common: sleep, dream, and trance all release the activity of the subconscious, the undermind; they tend to employ primary-process thinking, while waking mentation is secondary process—rational. But now look at the EEG records of the four states. Now it's the d-state, the trance, and the waking state that have a lot in common, while the s-state—sleep—is utterly different. And you can't get straight from trance into true d-state dreaming. The s-state must intervene. Normally, you only enter d-state four or five times a night, every hour or two, and only for a quarter of an hour at a time. The rest of the time you're in one stage or another of normal sleep. And there you'll dream, but usually not vividly; mentation in s-sleep is like an engine idling, a kind of steady muttering of images and thoughts. What we're after are the vivid, emotion-laden, memorable dreams of the d-state. Our hypnosis plus the Augmentor will ensure that we get them, get across the neurophysiological and temporal gulf of sleep, right into dreaming. So we'll need you on the couch here. My field was pioneered by Dement, Aserinsky, Berger, Oswald, Hartmann, and the rest, but the couch we get straight from Papa Freud. . . . But we use it to *sleep on,* which he objected to. Now, what I want, just for a starter, is for you to sit down here on the foot of the couch. Yes, that's it. You'll be there a while, so make yourself comfortable. You said you'd tried autohypnosis, didn't you? All right, Just go ahead and use the techniques you used for that. How about deep breathing? Count ten while you inhale, hold for five; yes, right, excellent. Would you mind looking up at the ceiling, straight up over your head. O.K., right."

As Orr obediently tipped his head back, Haber, close beside him, reached out quickly and quietly and put his left hand behind the man's head, pressing firmly with thumb and one finger behind and below each ear; at the same time with right thumb and finger he pressed hard on the bared throat, just below the soft, blond beard, where the vagus nerve and carotid artery run. He was aware of the fine, sallow skin under his fingers; he felt the first startled movement of protest, then saw the clear eyes closing. He felt a thrill of enjoyment of his own skill, his instant dominance over the patient, even as he was muttering softly and rapidly, "You're going to sleep now; close your eyes, sleep, relax, let your mind go blank; you're going to sleep, you're relaxed, you're going limp; relax, let go—"

And Orr fell backward on the couch like a man shot dead, his right hand dropping lax from his side.

Haber knelt by him at once, keeping his right hand lightly on the pressure spots and never stopping the quiet, quick flow of suggestion. "You're in trance now, not asleep but deeply in hypnotic trance, and you will not come out of it and awaken until I tell you to do so. You're in trance now, and going deeper all the time into trance, but you can still hear my voice and follow my instructions. After this, whenever I simply touch you on the throat as I'm doing now, you'll enter the hypnotic trance at once." He repeated the instructions, and went on. "Now when I tell you to open your eyes you'll do so, and see a crystal ball floating in front of you. I want you to fix your attention on it closely, and as you do so you will continue to go deeper into trance. Now open your eyes, yes, good, and tell me when you see the crystal ball."

The light eyes, now with a curious inward gaze, looked past Haber at nothing. "Now," the hypnotized man said very softly.

"Good. Keep gazing at it, and breathing regularly; soon you'll be in very deep trance. . . ."

Haber glanced up at the clock. The whole business had only taken a couple of minutes. Good; he didn't like to waste time on means, getting to the desired end was the thing. While Orr lay staring at his imaginary crystal ball, Haber got up and began fitting him with the modified trancap, constantly removing and replacing it to readjust the tiny electrodes and position them on the scalp under the thick, light-brown hair. He spoke often and softly, repeating suggestions and occasionally asking bland questions so that Orr would not drift off into sleep yet and would stay in rapport. As soon as the cap was in place he switched on the EEG, and for a while he watched it, to see what this brain looked like.

Eight of the cap's electrodes went to the EEG; inside the machine, eight pens scored a permanent record of the brain's electrical activity. On the screen which Haber watched, the impulses were reproduced directly, jittering white scribbles on dark gray. He could isolate and enlarge one, or superimpose one on another, at will. It was a scene he never tired of, the All-Night Movie, the show on Channel One.

There were none of the sigmoid jags he looked for, the concomitant of certain schizoid personality types. There was nothing unusual about the total pattern, except its diversity. A simple brain produces a relatively simple jig-jog set of patterns and is content to repeat them; this was not a simple brain. Its motions were subtle and complex, and the repetitions neither frequent nor unvaried. The computer of the Augmentor would analyze them, but until he saw the analysis Haber could isolate no singular factor except the complexity itself.

On commanding the patient to cease seeing the crystal ball and close his eyes, he obtained almost at once a strong, clear alpha trace at 12 cycles. He played about a little more with the brain, getting records for the computer and testing hynotic depth, and then said, "Now, John—" No, what the hell was the subject's name? "George. Now you're going to go to sleep in a minute. You're going to go sound asleep and dream; but you won't go to sleep until I say the word 'Antwerp'; when I say that, you'll go to sleep, and sleep until I say your name three times. Now when you sleep, you're going to have a dream, a good dream. One clear, pleasant dream. Not a bad dream at all, a pleasant one, but very clear and vivid. You'll be sure to remember it when you wake up. It will be about—" He hesitated a moment; he hadn't planned anything, relying on inspiration. "About a horse. A big bay horse galloping in a field. Running around. Maybe you'll ride the horse, or catch him, or maybe just watch him. But

25

the dream will be about a horse. A vivid—" what was the word the patient had used?—"*effective* dream about a horse. After that you won't dream anything else; and when I speak your name three times you'll wake up feeling calm and rested. Now, I am going to send you to sleep by . . . saying . . . Antwerp."

Obedient, the little dancing lines on the screen began to change. They grew stronger and slower; soon the sleep spindles of stage 2 sleep began to appear, and a hint of the long, deep delta rhythm of stage 4. And as the brain's rhythms changed, so did the heavy matter inhabited by that dancing energy: the hands were lax on the slow-breathing chest, the face was aloof and still.

The Augmentor had got a full record of the waking brain's patterns; now it was recording and analyzing the s-sleep patterns; soon it would be picking up the beginning of the patient's d-sleep patterns, and would be able even within this first dream to feed them back to the sleeping brain, amplifying its own emissions. Indeed it might be doing so now. Haber had expected a wait, but the hypnotic suggestion, plus the patient's long semideprivation of dreams, were putting him into the d-state at once: no sooner had he reached stage 2 than he began the re-ascent. The slowly swaying lines on the screen jittered once here and there; jigged again; began to quicken and dance, taking on a rapid, unsynchronized rhythm. Now the pons was active, and the trace from the hippocampus showed a five-second cycle, the theta rhythm, which had not showed up clearly in this subject. The fingers moved a little; the eyes under closed lids moved, watching; the lips parted for a deep breath. The sleeper dreamed.

It was 5:06.

At 5:11 Haber pressed the black OFF button on the Augmentor. At 5:12, noticing the deep jags and spindles of s-sleep reappearing, he leaned over the patient and said his name clearly thrice.

Orr sighed, moved his arm in a wide, loose gesture, opened his eyes, and wakened. Haber detached the electrodes from his scalp in a few deft motions. "Feel O.K.?" he asked, genial and assured.

"Fine."

"And you dreamed. That much I can tell you. Can you tell me the dream?"

"A horse," Orr said huskily, still bewildered by sleep. He sat up. "It was about a horse. That one," and he waved his hand toward the picture-window-size mural that decorated Haber's office, a photograph of the great racing stallion Tammany Hall at play in a grassy paddock.

"What did you dream about it?" Haber said, pleased. He had not been sure hypnosuggestion would work on dream content in a first hypnosis.

"It was. . . . I was walking in this field, and it was off in the distance for a while. Then it came galloping at me, and after a while I realized it was going to run me down. I wasn't scared at all, though. I figured perhaps I could catch its bridle, or swing up and ride it. I knew that actually it couldn't hurt me because it was the horse in your picture, not a real one. It was all a sort of game. . . . Dr. Haber, does anything about that picture strike you as . . . as unusual?"

"Well, some people find it overdramatic for a shrink's office, a bit overwhelming. A life-size sex symbol right opposite the couch!" He laughed.

"Was it there an hour ago? I mean, wasn't that a view of Mount Hood, when I came in—before I dreamed about the horse?"

Oh Christ it had been Mount Hood the man was right

It had not been Mount Hood it could not have been Mount Hood it was a horse it was a *horse*

It had been a mountain

A horse it was a horse it was—

He was staring at George Orr, staring blankly at him, several seconds must have passed since Orr's question, he must not be caught out, he must inspire confidence, he knew the answers.

"George, do you remember the picture there as being a photograph of Mount Hood?"

"Yes," Orr said in his rather sad but unshaken way. "I do. It was. Snow on it."

"Mhm," Haber nooded judicially, pondering. The awful chill at the pit of his chest had passed.

"You don't?"

The man's eyes, so elusive in color yet clear and direct in gaze: they were the eyes of a psychotic.

"No, I'm afraid I don't. It's Tammany Hall, the triple-winner back in '89. I miss the races, it's a shame the way the lower species get crowded out by our food problems. Of course a horse is the perfect anachronism, but I like the picture; it has vigor, strength—total self-realization in animal terms. It's a sort of ideal of what a psychiatrist strives to achieve in human psychological terms, a symbol. It's the source of my suggestion of your dream content, of course, I happened to be looking at it. . . ." Haber glanced sidelong at the mural. Of course it was the horse. "But listen, if you want a third opinion we'll ask Miss Crouch; she's worked here two years."

"She'll say it always was a horse," Orr said calmly but ruefully. "It always was. Since my dream. Always has been. I thought that maybe, since you suggested the dream to me, you might have the double memory, like me. But I guess you don't." But his eyes, no longer downcast, looked again at Haber with that clarity, that forbearance, that quiet and despairing plea for help.

The man was sick. He must be cured. "I'd like you to come again, George, and tomorrow if possible."

"Well, I work—"

"Get off an hour early, and come here at four. You're under VTT. Tell your boss, and don't feel any false shame about it. At one time or another 82 per cent of the population gets VTT, not to mention the 31 per cent that gets OTT. So be here at four and we'll get to work. We're going to get somewhere with this, you know. Now, here's a prescription for meprobamate; it'll keep your dreams low-keyed without suppressing the d-state entirely. You can refill it at the autodrug every three days. If you have a dream, or any other experience that frightens you, call me, day or night. But I doubt you will, using that; and if you're willing to work hard at this with me, you won't be needing any drug much longer. You'll have this whole problem with your dreams licked, and be out in the clear. Right?"

Orr took the IBM prescription card. "It would be a relief," he said. He smiled, a tentative, unhappy, yet not humorless smile. "Another thing about the horse," he said.

Haber, a head taller, stared down at him.

"It looks like you," Orr said.

Haber looked up quickly at the mural. It did. Big, healthy, hairy, reddish-brown, bearing down at a full gallop—

"Perhaps the horse in your dream resembled me?" he asked, shrewdly genial.

"Yes, it did," the patient said.

When he was gone, Haber sat down and looked up uneasily at the mural photograph of Tammany Hall. It really was too big for the office. Goddamn but he wished he could afford an office with a window with a view!

3

Those whom heaven helps we call the sons of heaven. They do not learn this by learning. They do not work it by working. They do not reason it by using reason. To let understanding stop at what cannot be understood is a high attainment. Those who cannot do it will be destroyed on the lathe of heaven.

—Chuang Tse: XXIII

George Orr left work at 3:30 and walked to the subway station; he had no car. By saving, he might have afforded a VW Steamer and the mileage tax on it, but what for? Downtown was closed to automobiles, and he lived downtown. He had learned to drive, back in the eighties, but had never owned a car. He rode the Vancouver subway back into Portland. The trains were already jam-packed; he stood out of reach of strap or stanchion, supported solely by the equalizing pressure of bodies on all sides, occasionally lifted right off his feet and floating as the force of crowding (c) exceeded the force of gravity (g). A man next to him holding a newspaper had never been able to lower his arms, but stood with his face muffled in the sports section. The headline, "BIG A-1 STRIKE NEAR AFGHAN BORDER," and the subhead, "Threat of Afghan Intervention," stared Orr eye to I for six stops. The newspaper-holder fought his way off and was replaced by a couple of tomatoes on a green plastic plate, beneath which was an old lady in a green plastic coat, who stood on Orr's left foot for three more stops.

He struggled off at the East Broadway stop, and shoved along for four blocks through the ever-thickening off-work

30

crowd to Willamette East Tower, a great, showy, shoddy shaft of concrete and glass competing with vegetable obstinacy for light and air with the jungle of similar buildings all around it. Very little light and air got down to street level; what there was was warm and full of fine rain. Rain was an old Portland tradition, but the warmth—70° F. on the second of March—was modern, a result of air pollution. Urban and industrial effluvia had not been controlled soon enough to reverse the cumulative trends already at work in the mid-Twentieth Century; it would take several centuries for the CO_2 to clear out of the air, if it ever did. New York was going to be one of the larger casualties of the Greenhouse Effect, as the polar ice kept melting and the sea kept rising; indeed all Boswash was imperiled. There were some compensations. San Francisco Bay was already on the rise, and would end up covering all the hundreds of square miles of landfill and garbage dumped into it since 1848. As for Portland, with eighty miles and the Coast Range between it and the sea, it was not threatened by rising water: only by falling water.

It had always rained in western Oregon, but now it rained ceaselessly, steadily, tepidly. It was like living in a downpour of warm soup, forever.

The New Cities—Umatilla, John Day, French Glen— were east of the Cascades, in what had been desert thirty years before. It was fiercely hot there still in summer, but it rained only 45 inches a year, compared with Portland's 114 inches. Intensive farming was possible: the desert blossomed. French Glen now had a population of 7 million. Portland, with only 3 million and no growth potential, had been left far behind in the March of Progress. That was nothing new for Portland. And what difference did it make? Undernourishment, overcrowding, and pervading foulness of the environment were the norm. There was more scurvy, typhus, and hepatitis in the Old Cities, more gang violence, crime, and murder in the New Cities. The rats ran one and the Mafia ran the other. George Orr styed in Portland because he had always lived there and because he had no reason to believe that life anywhere else would be better, or different.

Miss Crouch, smiling uninterestedly, showed him right in. Orr had thought that psychiatrists' offices, like rabbit holes, always had a front and a back door. This one didn't, but he doubted that patients were likely to run into one another coming and going, here. Up at the Medical School they had said that Dr. Haber had only a small psychiatric practice, being essentially a research man. That had given him the notion of someone successful and exclusive, and the doctor's jovial, masterful manner had confirmed it. But today, less nervous, he saw more. The office didn't have the platinum-and-leather assurance of financial success, nor the rag-and-bottle assurance of scientific disinterest. The chairs and couch were vinyl, the desk was metal plasticoated with a wood finish. Nothing whatever was genuine. Dr. Haber, white-toothed, bay-maned, huge, boomed out, "Good afternoon!"

That geniality was not faked, but it was exaggerated. There was a warmth to the man, an outgoingness, which was real; but it had got plasticoated with professional mannerisms, distorted by the doctor's unspontaneous use of himself. Orr felt in him a wish to be liked and a desire to be helpful; the doctor was not, he thought, really sure that anyone else existed, and wanted to prove they did by helping them. He boomed "Good afternoon!" so loud because he was never sure he would get an answer. Orr wanted to say something friendly, but nothing personal seemed suitable; he said, "It looks as if Afghanistan might get into the war."

"Mhm, that's been in the cards since last August." He should have known that the doctor would be better informed on world affairs than himself; he was generally semi-informed and three weeks out of date. "I don't think that'll shake the Allies," Haber went on, "unless it pulls Pakistan in on the Iranian side. Then India may have to send in more than token support to the Isragypts." That was teleglot for the New Arab Republic/Israel alliance. "I think Gupta's speech in Delhi shows that he's preparing for that eventuality."

"It keeps spreading," Orr said, feeling inadequate and despondent. "The war, I mean."

"Does it worry you?"

"Doesn't it worry you?"

"Irrelevant," said the doctor, smiling his broad, hairy, bear's smile, like a big bear-god; but he was still wary, since yesterday.

"Yes, it worries me." But Haber had not earned that answer; the questioner cannot withdraw himself from the question, assuming objectivity—as if the answers were an object. Orr did not speak these thoughts, however; he was in a doctor's hands, and surely the doctor knew what he was doing.

Orr had a tendency to assume that people knew what they were doing, perhaps because he generally assumed that he did not.

"Sleep well?" Haber inquired, sitting down under the left rear hoof of Tammany Hall.

"Fine, thanks."

"How do you feel about another go in the Palace of Dreams?" He was watching keenly.

"Sure, that's what I'm here for, I guess."

He saw Haber rise and come around the desk, he saw the large hand come out toward his neck, and then nothing happened.

". . . George . . ."

His name. Who called? No voice he know. Dry land, dry air, the crash of a strange voice in his ear. Daylight, and no direction. No way back. He woke.

The half-familiar room; the half-familiar, big man, in his voluminous russet gernreich, with his red-brown beard, and white smile, and opaque dark eyes. "It looked like a short dream but a lively one, on the EEG," said the deep voice. "Let's have it. Sooner the recall, the completer it is."

Orr sat up, feeling rather dizy. He was on the couch, how had he got there? "Let's see. It wasn't much. The horse again. Did you tell me to dream of the horse again, when I was hypnotized?"

Haber shook his head, meaning neither yes nor no, and listened.

"Well, this was a stable. This room. Straw and a manger

33

and a pitchfork in the corner, and so on. The horse was in it. He . . ."

Haber's expectant silence permitted no evasion.

"He did this tremendous pile of shit. Brown, steaming. Horseshit. It looked kind of like Mount Hood, with that little hump on the north side and everything. It was all over the rug, and sort of encroaching on me, so I said, 'It's only the picture of the mountain.' Then I guess I started to wake up."

Orr raised his face, looking past Dr. Haber at the mural behind him, the wall-sized photograph of Mount Hood.

It was a serene picture in rather muted, arty tones: the sky gray, the mountain a soft brown or reddish-brown, with speckles of white near the summit, and the foreground all dusky, formless treetops.

The doctor was not looking at the mural. He was watching Orr with those keen, opaque eyes. He laughed when Orr was done, not long or loudly, but perhaps a little excitedly.

"We're geeting somewhere, George!"

"Where?"

Orr felt rumpled and foolish, sitting on the couch still giddy from sleep, having lain asleep there, probably with his mouth open and snoring, helpless, while Haber watched the secret jigs and prancings of his brain, and told him what to dream. He felt exposed, used. And to what end?

Evidently the doctor had no memory at all of the horse-mural, nor of the conversation they had had concerning it; he was altogether in this new present, and all his memories led to it. So he could not do any good at all. But he was striding up and down the office now, talking even louder than usual. "Well! (a) you can and do dream to order, you follow the hypnosuggestions; (b) you respond splendidly to the Augmentor. Therefore we can work together, fast and efficiently, without narcosis. I'd rather work without drugs. What the brain does by itself is infinitely more fascinating and complex than any response it can make to chemical stimulation; that's why I developed the Augmentor, to provide the brain a means of *self*-stimulation. The creative and therapeutic resources of

34

the brain—whether waking or sleeping or dreaming—are practically infinite. If we can just find the keys to all the locks. The power of dreaming alone is quite undreamt of!" He laughed his big laugh, he had made that little joke many times. Orr smiled uncomfortably, it struck a bit close to home. "I am sure now that your therapy lies in this direction, to *use* your dreams, not to evade and avoid them. To face your fear and, with my help, see it through. You're afraid of your own mind, George, That's a fear no man can live with. But you don't have to. You haven't seen the help your own mind can give you, the ways you can use it, employ it creatively. All you need to do is not to hide from your own mental powers, not to suppress them, but to release them. This we can do together. Now, doesn't that strike you as right, as the right thing to do?"

"I don't know," Orr said.

When Haber spoke of using, employing his mental powers, he had thought for a moment that the doctor must mean his power of changing reality by dreaming; but surely if he'd meant that he would have said it clearly? Knowing that Orr desperately needed confirmation, he would not causelessly withhold it if he could give it.

Orr's heart sank. The use of narcotics and pep pills had left him emotionally off-balance; he knew that, and therefore kept trying to combat and control his feelings. But this disappointment was beyond his control. He had, he now realized, allowed himself a little hope. He had been sure, yesterday, that the doctor was aware of the change from mountain to horse. It hadn't surprised or alarmed him that Haber tried to hide his awareness, in the first shock; no doubt he had been unable to admit it even to himself, to encompass it. It had taken Orr himself a long time to bring himself to face the fact that he was doing something impossible. Yet he had let himself hope that Haber, knowing the dream, and being there as it was dreamed, at the center, might see the change, might remember and confirm.

No good. No way out. Orr was where he had been for months—alone: knowing he was insane and knowing he was not insane, simultaneously and intensely. It was enough to drive him insane.

"Would it be possible," he said diffidently, "for you to give me a posthypnotic suggestion not to dream effectively? Since you can suggest that I *do*. . . . That way I could get off drugs, at least for a while."

Haber settled down behind his desk, hunched like a bear. "I very much doubt it would work, even through one night," he said quite simply. And then suddenly booming again, "Isn't that the same fruitless direction you've been trying to go, George? Drugs or hypnosis, it's still suppression. You can't run away from your own mind. You see that, but you're not quite willing yet to face it. That's all right. Look at it this way: twice now you've dreamed, right here, on that couch. Was it so bad? Did it do any harm?"

Orr shook his head, too low-spirited to answer.

Haber went on talking, and Orr tried to give him his attention. He was talking now about daydreams, about their relationship to the hour-and-a-half dreaming cycles of the night, about their uses and value. He asked Orr if any particular type of daydream was congenial to him. "For example," he said, "I frequently daydream heroics. I am the hero. I'm saving a girl, or a fellow astronaut, or a besieged city, or a whole damn planet. Messiah dreams, do-gooder dreams. Haber saves the world! They're a hell of a lot of fun—so long as I keep 'em where they belong. We all need that ego boost we get from daydreams, but when we start relying on it, then our reality-parameters are getting a bit shaky. . . . Then there's the South Sea Island type daydreams—a lot of middle-aged executives go in for them. And the noble-suffering-martyr type, and the various romantic fantasies of adolescence, and the sado-masochist daydream, and so on. Most people recognize most types. We've almost all been in the arena facing the lions, at least once, or thrown a bomb and destroyed our enemies, or rescued the pneumatic virgin from the sinking ship, or written Beethoven's Tenth Symphony for him. Which style do you favor?"

"Oh—escape," Orr said. He really had to pull himself

together and answer this man, who was trying to help him. "Getting away. Getting out from under."

"Out from under the job, the daily grind?"

Haber seemed to refuse to believe that he was contented with his job. No doubt Haber had a lot of ambition and found it hard to believe that a man could be without it.

"Well, it's more the city, the crowding, I mean. Too many people everywhere. The headlines. Everything."

"South Seas?" Haber inquired with his bear's grin.

"No. Here. I'm not very imaginative. I daydream about having a cabin somewhere outside the cities, maybe over in the Coast Range where there's still some of the old forests."

"Ever considered actually buying one?"

"Recreation land is about thirty-eight thousand dollars an acre in the cheapest areas, down in the South Oregon Wilderness. Goes up to about four hundred thousand for a lot with a beach view."

Haber whistled. "I see you have considered—and so returned to your daydreams. Thank God they're free, eh! Well, are you game for another go? We've got nearly half an hour left."

"Could you . . ."

"What, George?"

"Let me keep recall."

Haber began one of his elaborate refusals. "Now as you know, what is experienced during hypnosis, including all directions given, is normally blocked to waking recall by a mechanism similar to that which blocks recall of 99 per cent of our dreams. To lower that block would be to give you too many conflicting directions concerning what is a fairly delicate matter, the content of a dream you haven't yet dreamed. That—the dream—I can direct you to recall. But I don't want your recall of my suggestions all mixed up with your recall of the dream you actually dream. I want to keep 'em separate, to get a clear report of what you did dream, not what you think you ought to have dreamed. Right? You can trust me, you know. I'm in this game to help you. I won't ask too much of you. I'll push you, but not too hard or too fast. I won't give you any nightmares! Believe me, I want to see this through, and understand it, as much as you do. You're an intelligent and cooperative subject, and a courageous man to have borne so much anxiety alone so long. We'll see this through, George. Believe me."

Orr did not entirely believe him, but he was an uncontradictable as a preacher; and besides, he wished he could believe him.

He said nothing, but lay back on the couch and submitted to the touch of the great hand on his throat.

"O.K.! There you are! What did you dream, George? Let's have it, hot off the griddle."

He felt sick and stupid.

"Something about the South Seas . . . coconuts . . . . Can't remember." He rubbed his head, scratched under his short beard, took a deep breath. He longed for a drink of cold water. "Then I . . . dreamed that you were walking with John Kennedy, the president, down Alder Street I think it was. I was sort of coming along behind, I think I was carrying something for one of you. Kennedy had his umbrella up—I saw him in profile, like the old fifty-cent pieces—and you said, 'You won't be needing that any more, Mr. President,' and took it out of his hand. He seemed to get annoyed over it, he said something I couldn't understand. But it had stopped raining, the sun came out, and so he said, 'I suppose you're right, now.' . . . It *has* stopped raining."

"How do you know?"

Orr sighed. "You'll see when you go out. Is that all for this afternoon?"

"I'm ready for more. Bill's on the Government, you know!"

"I'm very tired."

"Well, all right then, that wraps it up for today. Listen, what if we had our sessions at night? Let you go to sleep normally, use the hypnosis only to suggest dream content. It'd leave your working days clear, and my working day *is* night, half the time; one thing sleep researchers seldom do is sleep! It would speed us up tremendously, and save your

38

having to use any dream-suppressant drugs. You want to give it a try? How about Friday night?"

"I've got a date," Orr said and was startled at his lie.

"Saturday, then."

"All right."

He left, carrying his damp raincoat over his arm. There was no need to wear it. The Kennedy dream had been a strong effective. He was sure of them now, when he had them. No matter how bland their content, he woke from them recalling them with intense clarity, and feeling broken and abraded, as one might after making an enormous physical effort to resist an overwhelming, battering force. On his own, he had not had one oftener than once a month or once in six weeks; it had been the *fear* of having one that had obsessed him. Now, with the Augmentor keeping him in dreaming-sleep, and the hypnotic suggestions insisting that he dream effectively, he had had three effective dreams out of four in two days; or, discounting the coconut dream, which had been rather what Haber called a mere muttering of images, three out of three. He was exhausted.

It was not raining. When he came out of the portals of Willamette East Tower, the March sky was high and clear above the street canyons. The wind had come round to blow from the east, the dry desert wind that from time to time enlivened the wet, hot, sad, gray weather of the Valley of the Willamette.

The clearer air roused his spirits a bit. He straightened his shoulders and set off, trying to ignore a faint dizziness that was probably the combined result of fatigue, anxiety, two brief naps at an unusual time of day, and a sixty-two-story descent by elevator.

Had the doctor told him to dream that it had stopped raining? Or had the suggestion been to dream about Kennedy (who had, now that he thought about it again, had Abraham Lincoln's beard)? Or about Haber himself? He had no way of telling. The effective part of the dream had been the stopping of the rain, the change of weather; but that proved nothing. Often it was not the apparently striking or salient element of a dream which was the effective one. He suspected that Kennedy, for reasons known only to his subconscious mind, had been his own addition, but he could not be sure.

He went down into the East Broadway subway station with the endless others. He dropped his five-dollar piece in the ticket machine, got his ticket, got his train, entered darkness under the river.

The dizziness increased in his body and in his mind.

To go under a river: there's a strange thing to do, a really weird idea.

To cross a river, ford it, wade it, swim it, use boat, ferry, bridge, airplane, to go upriver, to go downriver in the ceaseless renewal and beginning of current: all that makes sense. But in going under a river, something is involved which is, in the central meaning of the word, perverse. There are roads in the mind and outside it the mere elaborateness of which shows plainly that, to have got into this, a wrong turning must have been taken way back.

There were nine train and truck tunnels under the Willamette, sixteen bridges across it, and concrete banks along it for twenty-seven miles. Flood control on both it and its great confluent the Columbia, a few miles downstream from central Portland, was so highly developed that neither river could rise more than five inches even after the most prolonged torrential rains. The Willamette was a useful element of the environment, like a very large, docile draft animal harnessed with straps, chains, shafts, saddles, bits, girths, hobbles. If it hadn't been useful of course it would have been concreted over, like the hundreds of little creeks and streams that ran in darkness down from the hills of the city under the streets and buildings. But without it, Portland would not have been a port; the ships, the long strings of barges, the big rafts of lumber still came up and down it. So the trucks and trains and the few private cars had to go over the river or under it. Above the heads of those now riding the GPRT train in the Broadway Tunnel were tons of rock and gravel, tons of water running, the piles of wharves and the keels of ocean-going ships, the huge concrete supports of elevated freeway bridges and approaches, a convoy of steamer trucks laden with frozen battery-produced chickens, one jet plane at 34,000 feet, the stars at 4.3 + light-years. George Orr, pale in the flickering fluorescent glare of the train car in the infrafluvial dark, swayed as he stood holding a swaying steel handle on a strap among a thousand other souls. He felt the heaviness upon him, the weight bearing down endlessly. He thought, I am living in a nightmare, from which from time to time I wake in sleep.

The smash and jostle of people getting off at the Union Station stop knocked this sententious notion out of his mind; he concentrated wholly on keeping hold of the handle on the strap. Still feeling giddy, he was afraid that if he lost hold and had to submit entirely to force (c), he might get sick.

The train started up again with a noise evenly compounded of deep abrasive roars and high piercing screams.

The whole GPRT system was only fifteen years old, but it had been built late and hastily, with inferior materials, during, not before, the crack-up of the private car economy. In fact the train cars had been built in Detroit; and they lasted like it, and sounded like it. A city man and subway rider, Orr did not even hear the appalling noise. His aural nerve endings were in fact considerably dulled in sensitivity though he was only thirty, and in any case the noise was merely the usual background of the nightmare. He was thinking again, having established his claim to the handle of the strap.

Ever since he had got interested in the subject perforce, the mind's lack of recall of most dreams had puzzled him. Nonconscious thinking, whether in infancy or in dream, apparently is not available to conscious recall. But was he unconscious during hypnosis? Not at all: wide awake, until told to sleep. Why could he not remember, then? It worried him. He wanted to know what Haber was doing. The first dream this afternoon, for example: Had the doctor merely told him to dream about the horse again? And he himself had added the horseshit, which was embarrassing. Or, if the doctor had specified the horseshit, that was embarrassing in a different way. And perhaps Haber was lucky that he hadn't ended up with a big brown

41

steaming pile of manure on the office carpeting. In a sense, of course, he had: the picture of the mountain.

Orr stood upright as if he had been goosed, as the train screamed into Alder Street Station. The mountain, he thought, as sixty-eight people pushed and shoved and scraped past him to the doors. The mountain. He told me to put back the mountain in my dream. So I had the horse put back the mountain. But if he told me to put back the mountain then he *knew it had been there before the horse.* He knew. He did see the first dream change reality. He saw the change. He believes me. I am *not* insane!

So great a joy filled Orr that, among the forty-two persons who had been jamming into the car as he thought these things, the seven or eight pressed closest to him felt a slight but definite glow of benevolence or relief. The woman who had failed to get his strap handle away from him felt a blessed surcease of the sharp pain in her corn; the man squashed against him on the left thought suddenly of sunlight; the old man sitting crouched directly in front of him forgot, for a little, that he was hungry.

Orr was not a fast reasoner. In fact, he was not a reasoner. He arrived at ideas the slow way, never skating over the clear, hard ice of logic, nor soaring on the slip-streams of imagination, but slogging, plodding along on the heavy ground of existence. He did not see connections, which is said to be the hallmark of intellect. He *felt* connections—like a plumber. He was not really a stupid man, but he did not use his brains half as much as he might have done, or half as fast. It was not until he had got off the subway at Ross Island Bridge West, and had walked up the hill several blocks and taken the elevator eighteen floors to his one-room 8½ X 11 flat in the twenty-story independent-income steel-and-sleazy-concrete Corbett Condominium (Budget Living in Style Down Town!), and had put a soybeanloaf slice in the infrabake, and had taken a beer out of the wallfridge, and had stood some while at his window—he paid double for an outside room—looking up at the West Hills of Portland crammed with huge glittering towers, heavy with lights and life, that he thought at last: Why didn't Dr. Haber *tell* me that he knows I dream effectively?

He mulled over this a while. He slogged around it, tried to lift it, found it very bulky.

He thought: Haber knows, now, that the mural has changed twice. Why didn't he say anything? He must know I was afraid of being insane. He says he's helping me. It would have helped a lot if he'd told me that he can see what I see, told me that it's not just delusion.

He knows now, Orr thought after a long slow swallow of beer, that it's stopped raining. He didn't go to see, though, when I told him it had. Maybe he was afraid to. That's probably it. He's scared by this whole thing and wants to find out more before he tells me what he really thinks about it. Well, I can't blame him. If he weren't scared of it, that would be the odd thing.

But I wonder, once he gets used to the idea, what he'll do. . . . I wonder how he'll stop my dreams, how he'll keep me from changing things. I've got to stop; this is far enough, far enough. . . .

He shook his head and turned away from the bright, life-encrusted hills.

4

> Nothing endures, nothing is precise and certain
> (except the mind of a pedant), perfection is the
> mere repudiation of that ineluctable marginal
> inexactitude which is the mysterious inmost quality
> of Being.
>
> —H. G. Wells, *A Modern Utopia*

The law office of Forman, Esserbeck, Goodhue and Rutti was in a 1973 automobile parking structure, converted to human use. Many of the older buildings of downtown Portland were of this lineage. At one time indeed most of downtown Portland had consisted of places to park automobiles. At first these had mostly been plains of asphalt punctuated by paybooths or parking meters, but as the population went up, so had they. Indeed the automatic-elevator parking structure had been invented in Portland, long long ago; and before the private car strangled in its own exhaust, ramp-style parking buildings had gone up to fifteen and twenty stories. Not all these had been torn down since the eighties to make room for high-rise office and apartment buildings; some had been converted. This one, 209 S.W. Burnside, still smelled of ghostly gasoline fumes. Its cement floors were stained with the excreta of innumerable engines, the wheelprints of the dinosaurs were fossilized in the dust of its echoing halls. All the floors had a curious slant, a skewness, due to the basic helical-ramp construction of the building; in the offices of Forman, Esserbeck, Goodhue and Rutti, one was never entirely convinced that one was standing quite upright.

Miss Lelache sat behind the screen of bookcases and

files that semi-separated her semi-office from Mr. Pearl's semi-office, and thought of herself as a Black Widow.

There she sat, poisonous; hard, shiny, and poisonous; waiting, waiting.

And the victim came.

A born victim. Hair like a little girl's, brown and fine, little blond beard; soft white skin like a fish's belly; meek, mild, stuttering. Shit! If she stepped on him he wouldn't even crunch.

"Well I, I think it's a, it's a matter of, of rights of privacy sort of," he was saying. "Invasion of privacy, I mean. But I'm not sure. That's why I wanted advice."

"Well. Shoot," said Miss Lelache.

The victim could not shoot. His stuttering pipe had dried up.

"You're under Voluntary Therapeutic Treatment," Miss Lelache said, referring to the note Mr. Esserbeck had sent in previously, "for infraction of Federal regulations controlling dispensation of medications at autodrugstores."

"Yes. If I agree to psychiatric treatment I won't get prosecuted."

"That's the gist of it, yes," the lawyer said dryly. The man struck her as not exactly feeble-minded, but revoltingly simple. She cleared her throat.

He cleared his throat. Monkey see, monkey do.

Gradually, with a lot of backing and filling, he explained that he was undergoing a therapy which consisted essentially of hypnotically induced sleep and dreaming. He felt that the psychiatrist, by ordering him to dream certain dreams, might be infringing upon his rights of privacy as defined in the New Federal Constitution of 1984.

"Well. Something like this came up last year in Arizona," said Miss Lelache. "Man under VTT tried to sue his therapist for implanting homosexual tendencies in him. Of course the shrink was simply using standard conditioning techniques, and the plaintiff actually was a terrific repressed homo; he got arrested for trying to bugger a twelve-year-old boy in broad daylight in the middle of Phoenix Park, before the case even got to court. He wound up in Obligatory Therapy in Tehachapi. Well. What I'm

45

getting at is that you've got to be cautious in making this sort of allegation. Most psychiatrists who get Government referrals are cautious men themselves, respectable practitioners. Now if you can provide any instance, any occurrence, that might serve as real evidence; but mere suspicions won't do. In fact, they might land you in Obligatory, that's the Mental Hospital in Linnton, or in jail."

"Could they . . . maybe just give me another psychiatrist?"

"Well. Not without real cause. The Medical School referred you to this Haber; and they're good, up there, you know. If you brought a complaint against Haber the men who heard it as specialists would very likely be Med School men, probably the same ones that interviewed you. They won't take a patient's word against a doctor's with no evidence. Not in this kind of case."

"A mental case," the client said sadly.

"Exactly."

He said nothing for a while. At last he raised his eyes to hers, clear, light eyes, a look without anger and without hope; he smiled and said, "Thank you very much, Miss Lelache. I'm sorry to have wasted your time."

"Well, wait!" she said. He might be simple, but he certainly didn't look crazy; he didn't even look neurotic. He just looked desperate. "You don't have to give up quite so easily. I didn't say that you have no case. You say that you do want to get off drugs, and that Dr. Haber is giving you a heavier dose of phenobarb, now, than you were taking on your own; that might warrant investigation. Though I strongly doubt it. But defense of rights of privacy is my special line, and I want to know if there's been a breach of privacy. I just said you hadn't *told* me your case—if you have one. What, specifically, has this doctor done?"

"If I tell you," the client said with mournful objectivity, "you'll think I'm crazy."

"How do you know I will?"

Miss Lelache was countersuggestible, an excellent quality in a lawyer, but she knew she carried it a bit far.

46

"If I told you," the client said in the same tone, "that some of my dreams exert an influence over reality, and that Dr. Haber has discovered this and is using it . . . this talent of mine, for ends of his own, without my consent . . . you'd think I was crazy. Wouldn't you?"

Miss Lelache gazed at him a while, her chin on her hands. "Well. Go on," she said at last, sharply. He was quite right about what she was thinking, but damned if she was going to admit it. Anyway, so what if he was crazy? What sane person could live in this world and not be crazy?

He looked down at his hands for a minute, evidently trying to collect his thoughts. "You see," he said, "he has this machine. A device like the EEG recorder, but it provides a kind of analysis and feedback of the brain waves."

"You mean he's a Mad Scientist with an Infernal Machine?"

The client smiled feebly. "I make it sound that way. No, I believe that he has a very good reputation as a research scientist, and that he's genuinely dedicated to helping people. I'm sure he doesn't intend any harm to me or anyone. His motives are very high." He encountered the disenchanted gaze of the Black Widow a moment, and stuttered. "The, the machine. Well, I can't tell you how it works, but anyway he's using it on me to keep my brain in the d-state, as he calls it—that's one term for the kind of special sleep you have when you're dreaming. It's quite different from ordinary sleep. He sends me to sleep hypnotically, and then turns this machine on so that I start dreaming at once—one doesn't usually. Or that's how I understand it. The machine makes sure that I dream, and I think it intensifies the dream-state, too. And then I dream what he's told me to dream in hypnosis."

"Well. It sounds like a foolproof method for an old-fashioned psychoanalyst to get dreams to analyze. But instead of that he's telling you what to dream, by hypnotic suggestion? So I assume he's conditioning you via dreams, for some reason. Now, it's well established that under hypnotic suggestion a person can and will do almost anything, whether or not his conscience would permit it in a normal state: that's been known since the middle of the last century, and legally established since *Somerville* v. *Projansky* in '88. Well. Do you have any grounds for believing that this doctor has been using hypnosis to suggest that you perform anything dangerous, anything you'd find it morally repugnant to do?"

The client hesitated. "Dangerous, yes. If you accept that a dream can be dangerous. But he doesn't direct me to *do* anything. Only to *dream* them."

"Well, are the dreams he suggests morally repugnant to you?"

"He's not . . . not an evil man. He means well. What I object to is his using me as an instrument, a means—even if his ends are good. I can't judge him—my own dreams had immoral effects, that's why I tried to suppress them with drugs, and got into this mess. And I want to get out of it, to get off drugs, to be cured. But he's not curing me. He's *encouraging* me."

After a pause, Miss Lelache said, "To do what?"

"To change reality by dreaming that it's different," the client said, doggedly, without hope.

Miss Lelache sank the point of her chin between her hands again and stared for a while at the blue clipbox on her desk at the very nadir of her range of vision. She glanced up surreptitiously at the client. There he sat, mild as ever, but she now thought that he certainly wouldn't squash if she stepped on him, nor crunch, nor even crack. He was peculiarly solid.

People who come to a lawyer tend to be on the defensive if not on the offensive; they are, naturally, out for something—a legacy, a property, an injunction, a divorce, a committal, whatever. She could not figure what this fellow, so inoffensive and defenseless, was out for. He made no sense at all and yet he didn't *sound* as if he wasn't making sense.

"All right," she said cautiously. "So what's wrong with what he's making your dreams do?"

"I have no right to change things. Nor he to make me do it."

48

God, he really believed it, he was completely off the deep end. And yet his moral certainty hooked her, as if she were a fish swimming around in the deep end, too.

"Change things how? What things? Give me an example!" She felt no mercy for him; as she should have felt for a sick man, a schiz or paranoid with delusions of manipulating reality. Here was "another casualty of these times of ours that try men's souls," as President Merdle, with his happy faculty for fouling a quotation, had said in his State of the Union message; and here she was being mean to a poor lousy bleeding casualty with holes in his brain. But she didn't feel like being kind to him. He could take it.

"The cabin," he said, having pondered a little. "My second visit to him, he was asking about daydreams, and I told him that sometimes I had daydreams about having a place in the Wilderness Areas, you know, a place in the country like in old novels, a place to get away to. Of course I didn't have one. Who does? But last week, he must have directed me to dream that I did. Because now I do. A thirty-three-year lease cabin on Government land, over in the Siuslaw National Forest, near the Neskowin. I rented a batcar and drove over Sunday to see it. It's very nice. But . . ."

"Why shouldn't you have a cabin? Is that immoral? Lots of people have been getting into those lotteries for those leases since they opened up some of the Wilderness Areas for them last year. You're just lucky as hell."

"But I didn't have one," he said. "Nobody did. The Parks and Forests were reserved strictly as wilderness, what there is left of them, with camping only around the borders. There were no Government-lease cabins. Until last Friday. When I dreamed that there were."

"But look, Mr. Orr, I *know*—"

" I know you know," he said gently. "I know, too. All about how they decided to lease parts of the National Forests last spring. And I applied, and got a winning number in the lottery, and so on. Only I also know that that was not true until last Friday. And Dr. Haber knows it, too."

"Then your dream last Friday," she said, jeering,

"changed reality retrospectively for the entire State of Oregon and affected a decision in Washington last year and erased everybody's memory but yours and your doctor's? Some dream! Can you remember it?"

"Yes," he said, morose but firm. "It was about the cabin, and the creek that's in front of it. I don't expect you to believe all this, Miss Lelache. I don't think even Dr. Haber has really caught on to it yet; he won't wait and get the feel of it. If he did, he might be more cautious about it. You see, it works like this. If he told me under hypnosis to dream that there was a pink dog in the room, I'd do it; but the dog couldn't be there so long as pink dogs aren't in the order of nature, aren't part of reality. What would happen is, either I'd get a white poodle dyed pink, and some plausible reason for its being there, or, if he insisted that it be a genuine pink dog, then my dream would have to change the order of nature to include pink dogs. Everywhere. Since the Pleistocene or whenever dogs first appeared. They would always have come black, brown, yellow, white, and pink. And one of the pink ones would have wandered in from the hall, or would be his collie, or his receptionist's Pekinese, or something. Nothing miraculous. Nothing unnatural. Each dream covers its tracks completely. There would just be a normal everyday pink dog there when I woke up, with a perfectly good reason for being there. And nobody would be aware of anything new, except me—and him. I keep the two memories, of the two realities. So does Dr. Haber. He's there at the moment of change, and knows what the dream's about. He doesn't admit that he knows, but I know he does. For everybody else, there have always been pink dogs. For me, and him, there have—and there haven't."

"Dual time-tracks, alternate universes," Miss Lelache said. "Do you see a lot of old late-night TV shows?"

"No," said the client, almost as dryly as she. "I don't ask you to believe this. Certainly not without evidence."

"Well. Thank God!"

He smiled, almost a laugh. He had a kind face; he looked, for some reason, as if he liked her.

"But look, Mr. Orr, how the hell can I get any evidence

50

about your *dreams?* Particularly if you destroy all the evidence every time you dream by changing everything ever since the Pleistocene?"

"Can you," he said, suddenly intense, as if hope had come to him, "can you, acting as my lawyer, ask to be present at one of my sessions with Dr. Haber—if you were willing?"

"Well. Possibly. It could be managed, if there's good cause. But look, calling in a lawyer as witness in the event of a possible privacy-infringement case is going to absolutely wreck your therapist-patient relationship. Not that it sounds like you've got a very good one going, but that's hard to judge from outside. The fact is, you have to trust him, and also, you know, he has to trust you, in a way. If you throw a lawyer at him because you want to get him out of your head, well, what can he do? Presumably he's trying to help you."

"Yes. But he's using me for experimental—" Orr got no further: Miss Lelache had stiffened, the spider had seen, at last, her prey.

"Experimental purposes? Is he? What? This machine you talked about—is it experimental? Has it HEW approval? What have you signed, any releases, anything beyond the VTT forms and the hypnosis-consent form? Nothing? That sounds like you might have just cause for complaint, Mr. Orr."

"You might be able to come observe a session?"

"Maybe. The line to follow would be civil rights, of course, not privacy."

"You do understand that I'm not trying to get Dr. Haber into trouble?" he said, looking worried. "I don't want to do that. I know he means well. It's just that I want to be cured, not used."

"If his motives are good, and if he's using an experimental device on a human subject, then he should take it quite as a matter of course, without resentment; if it's on the level, he won't get into any trouble. I've done jobs like this twice. Hired by HEW to do it. Watched a new hypnosis-inducer in practice up at the Med School, it didn't work, and watched a demonstration of how to

51

induce agoraphobia by suggestion, so people will be happy in crowds, out at the Institute in Forest Grove. That one worked but didn't get approved, it came under the brainwashing laws, we decided. Now, I can probably get an HEW order to investigate this thingummy your doctor's using. That lets you out of the picture. I don't come on as your lawer at all. In fact maybe I don't even know you. I'm an official accredited ACLU observer for HEW. Then, if we don't get anywhere with this, that leaves you and him in the same relationship as before. The only catch is, I've got to get invited to one of *your* sessions."

"I'm the only psychiatric patient he's using the Augmentor on, he told me so. He said he's still working on it—perfecting it."

"It really is experimental, whatever he's doing to you with it, then. Good. All right. I'll see what I can do. It'll take a week or more to get the forms through."

He looked distressed.

"You won't dream me out of existence this week, Mr. Orr," she said, hearing her chitinous voice, clicking her mandibles.

"Not willingly," he said, with gratitude—no, by God, it wasn't gratitude, it was liking. He liked her. He was a poor damn crazy psycho on drugs, he *would* like her. She liked him. She stuck out her brown hand, he met it with a white one, just like that damn button her mother always kept in the bottom of her bead box, SCNN or SNCC or something she'd belonged to way back in the middle of the last century, the Black hand and the White hand joined together. Christ!

5

When the Great Way is lost, we get benevolence and righteousness.

—Lao Tse: XVIII

Smiling, William Haber strode up the steps of the Oregon Oneirological Institute and through the high, polarized-glass doors into the dry cool of the air conditioning. It was only March 24, and already like a sauna-bath outside; but within all was cool, clean, serene. Marble floor, discreet furniture, reception desk of brushed chrome, well-enameled receptionist: "Good morning, Dr. Haber!"

In the hall Atwood passed him, coming from the research wards, red-eyed and tousled from a night of monitoring sleepers' EEG's; the computers did a lot of that now, but there were still times an unprogrammed mind was needed. "Morning, Chief," Atwood mumbled.

And from Miss Crouch in his own office, *"Good* morning, Doctor!" He was glad he'd brought Penny Crouch with him when he moved to the office of Director of the Institute last year. She was loyal and clever, and a man at the head of a big and complex research institution needs a loyal and clever woman in his outer office.

He strode on into the inner sanctum.

Dropping briefcase and file folders on the couch, he stretched his arms, and then went over, as he always did when he first entered his office, to the window. It was a large corner window, looking out east and north over a great sweep of world: the curve of the much-bridged Willamette close in beneath the hills; the city's countless towers high and milky in the spring mist, on either side of

53

the river; the suburbs receding out of sight till from their remote outbacks the foothills rose; and the mountains. Hood, immense yet withdrawn, breeding clouds about her head; going northward, the distant Adams, like a molar tooth; and then the pure cone of St. Helens, from whose long gray sweep of slope still farther northward a little bald dome stuck out, like a baby looking round its mother's skirt: Mount Rainier.

It was an inspiring view. It never failed to inspire Dr. Haber. Besides, after a week's solid rain, barometric pressure was up and the sun was out again, above the river mist. Well aware from a thousand EEG readings of the links between the pressure of the atmosphere and the heaviness of the mind, he could almost feel his psychosoma being buoyed up by that bright, drying wind. Have to keep that up, keep the climate improving, he thought rapidly, almost surreptitiously. There were several chains of thought formed or forming in his mind simultaneously, and this mental note was not part of any of them. It was quickly made and as quickly filed away in memory, even as he snapped on his desk recorder and began to dictate one of the many letters that the running of a Government-connected science research institute entailed. It was hackwork, of course, but it had to be done, and he was the man to do it. He did not resent it, though it cut drastically into his own research time. He was in the labs only for five or six hours a week now, usually, and had only one patient of his own, though of course he was supervising the therapy of several others.

One patient, however, he did keep. He was a psychiatrist, after all. He had gone into sleep research and oneirology in the first place to find therapeutic applications. He was not interested in detached knowledge, science for science' sake: there was no use learning anything if it was of no use. Relevance was his touchstone. He would always keep one patient of his own, to remind him of that fundamental commitment, to keep him in contact with the human reality of his research in terms of the disturbed personality structure of individual people. For there is nothing important except people. A person is defined solely by the extent of his influence over other people, by the sphere of his interrelationships; and morality is an utterly meaningless term unless defined as the good one does to others, the fulfilling of one's function in the sociopolitical whole.

His current patient, Orr, was coming in at four this afternoon, for they had given up the attempt at night sessions; and, as Miss Crouch reminded him at lunch time, an HEW inspector was going to observe today's session, making sure there was nothing illegal, immoral, unsafe, unkind, unetc., about the operation of the Augmentor. God damn Government prying.

That was the trouble with success, and its concomitants of publicity, public curiosity, professional envy, peer-group rivalry. If he'd still been a private researcher, plugging along in the sleep lab at P.S.U. and a second-rate office in Willamette East Tower, chances were that nobody would have taken any notice of his Augmentor until he decided it was ready to market, and he would have been let alone to refine and perfect the device and its applications. Now here he was doing the most private and delicate part of his business, psychotherapy with a disturbed patient, so the Government had to send a lawyer barging in not understanding half of what went on and misunderstanding the rest.

The lawyer arrived at 3:45, and Haber came striding into the outer office to greet him—her, it turned out—and to get a friendly warm impression established right away. It went better if they saw you were unafraid, cooperative, and personally cordial. A lot of doctors let their resentment show when they had an HEW inspector; and those doctors did not get many Government grants.

It was not altogether easy to be cordial and warm with this lawyer. She snapped and clicked. Heavy brass snap catch on handbag, heavy copper and brass jewelry that clattered, clump-heel shoes, and a huge silver ring with a horribly ugly African mask design, frowning eyebrows, hard voice: clack, clash, snap. . . . In the second ten seconds, Haber suspected that the whole affair was indeed a mask, as the ring said: a lot of sound and fury signifying

55

timidity. That, however, was none of his business. He would never know the woman behind the mask, and she did not matter, so long as he could make the right impression on Miss Lelache the lawyer.

If it didn't go cordially, at least it didn't go badly; she was competent, had done this kind of thing before, and had done her homework for this particular job. She knew what to ask and how to listen.

"This patient, George Orr," she said, "he's not an addict, correct? Is he diagnosed as psychotic or disturbed, after three weeks' therapy?"

"Disturbed, as the Health Office defines the word. Deeply disturbed and with artificial reality-orientations, but improving under current therapy."

She had a pocket recorder and was taking all this down: every five seconds, as the law required, the thing went *teep*.

"Will you describe the therapy you're employing please, *teep* and explain the role this device plays in it? Don't tell me how it *teep* works, that's in your report, but what it does. *Teep* for instance, how does its use differ from the Elektroson or the trancap?"

"Well, those devices, as you know, generate various low-frequency pulses which stimulate nerve cells in the cerebral cortex. Those signals are what you might call generalized; their effect on the brain is obtained in a manner basically similar to that of strobe lights at a critical rhythm, or an aural stimulus like a drumbeat. The Augmentor delivers a specific signal which can be picked up by a specific area. For instance, a subject can be trained to produce alpha rhythm at will, as you know; but the Augmentor can induce it without any training, and even when he's in a condition not normally conducive to the alpha rhythm. It feeds a 9-cycle alpha rhythm through appropriately placed electrodes, and within seconds the brain can accept that rhythm and begin producing alpha waves as steadily as a Zen Buddhist in trance. Similarly, and more usefully, any stage of sleep can be induced, with its typical cycles and regional activities."

56

"Will it stimulate the pleasure center, or the speech center?"

Oh, the moralistic gleam in an ACLU eye, whenever that pleasure-center bit came up! Haber concealed all irony and irritation, and answered with friendly sincerity, "No. It's not like ESB, you see. It's not like electrical stimulation, or chemical stimulation, of any center; it involves no intrusion on special areas of the brain. It simply induces the entire brain activity to change, to shift into another of its own, natural states. It's a bit like a catchy tune that sets your feet tapping. So the brain enters and maintains the condition desired for study or therapy, as long as need be I called it the Augmentor to point up its noncreative function. Nothing is imposed from outside. Sleep induced by the Augmentor is precisely, literally, the kind and quality of sleep normal to that particular brain. The difference between it and the electrosleep machines is like a personal tailor compared to mass-produced suits. The difference between it and electrode implantation is—oh, hell—a scalpel to a sledgehammer!"

"But how do you make up the stimuli you use? Do you *teep* record an alpha rhythm, for instance, from one subject to use on another *teep*?"

He had been evading this point. He did not intend to lie, of course, but there was simply no use talking about uncompleted research till it was done and tested; it might give a quite wrong impression to a nonspecialist. He launched into an answer easily, glad to hear his own voice instead of her snapping and bangle-clattering and teeping; it was curious how he only heard the annoying little sound when she was talking. "At first I used a generalized set of stimuli, averaged out from records of many subjects. The depressive patient mentioned in the report was treated successfully thus. But I felt the effects were more random and erratic than I liked. I began to experiment. On animals, of course. Cats. We sleep researchers like cats, you know; they sleep a lot! Well, with animal subjects I found that the most promising line was to use rhythms previously recorded from the subject's own brain. A kind of auto-stimulation via recordings. Specificity is what I'm after, you see. A brain will respond to its own alpha rhythm at once, and spontaneously. Now of course there are therapeutic vistas opened up along the other line of research. It might be possible to impose a slightly different pattern gradually upon the patient's own: a healthier or completer pattern. One recorded previously from that subject, possibly, or from a different subject. This could prove tremendously helpful in cases of brain damage, lesion, trauma; it might aid a damaged brain to re-establish its old habits in new channels—something which the brain struggles long and hard to do by itself. It might be used to 'teach' an abnormally functioning brain new habits, and so forth. However, that's all speculative, at this point, and if and when I return to research on that line I will of course reregister with HEW." That was quite true. There was no need to mention that he was doing research along that line, since so far it was quite inconclusive and would merely be misunderstood. "The form of autostimulation by recording that I'm using in this therapy may be described as having no effect on the patient beyond that exerted during the period of the machine's functioning: five to ten minutes." He knew more of any HEW lawyer's specialty than she knew of his; he saw her nodding slightly at that last sentence, it was right down her alley.

But then she said, "What *does* it do, then?"

"Yes, I was coming to that," Haber said, and quickly readjusted his tone, since the irritation was showing through. "What we have in this case is a subject who is afraid to dream: an oneirophobe. My treatment is basically a simple conditioning treatment in the classic tradition of modern psychology. The patient is induced to dream here, under controlled conditions; dream content and emotional affect are manipulated by hypnotic suggestion. The subject is being taught that he can dream safely, pleasantly, et cetera, a positive conditioning which will leave him free of his phobia. The Augmentor is an ideal instrument for this purpose. It ensures that he will dream, by instigating and then reinforcing his own typical d-state activity. It might take a subject up to an hour and a half to go through the various stages of s-sleep and reach the d-state on his own, an impractical length for daytime therapy sessions, and moreover during deep sleep the force of hypnotic suggestions concerning dream content might be partly lost. This is undesirable; while he's in conditioning, it's essential that he have no bad dreams, no nightmares. Therefore the Augmentor provides me with both a time-saving device and a safety factor. The therapy could be achieved without it; but it would probably take months; with it, I except to take a few weeks. It may prove to be as great a timesaver, in appropriate cases, as hypnosis itself has proved to be in psychoanalysis and in conditioning therapy."

Teep, said the lawyer's recorder, and *Bong* said his own desk communicator in a soft, rich, authoritative voice. Thank God. "Here's our patient now. Now I suggest, Miss Lelache, that you meet him, and we may chat a bit if you like; then perhaps you can fade off to that leather chair in the corner, right? Your presence shouldn't make any real difference to the patient, but if he's constantly reminded of it, it could slow things down badly. He's a person in a fairly severe anxiety state, you see, with a tendency to interpret events as personally threatening, and a set of protective delusions built up—as you'll see. Oh yes, and the recorder off, that's right, a therapy session's not for the record. Right? O.K., good. Yes, hello, George, come on in! This is Miss Lelache, the participant from HEW. She's here to see the Augmentor in use." The two were shaking hands in the most ridiculously stiff way. Crash clank! went the lawyer's bracelets. The contrast amused Haber: the harsh fierce woman, the meek characterless man. They had nothing in common at all.

"Now," he said, enjoying running the show, "I suggest that we get on with business, unless there's anything special on your mind, George, that you want to talk about first?" He was, by his own apparently unassertive movements, sorting them out: the Lelache to the chair in the far corner, Orr to the couch. "O.K., then, good. Let's run off a dream. Which will incidentally constitute a record for HEW of the fact that the Augmentor doesn't loosen your toenails, or harden your arteries, or blow your mind, or indeed have any side effects whatsoever except per-

59

haps a slight compensatory decrease in dreaming sleep tonight." As he finished the sentence he reached out and placed his right hand on Orr's throat, almost casually.

Orr flinched from the contact as if he had never been hypnotized.

Then he apologized. "Sorry. You come at me so suddenly."

It was necessary to rehypnotize him completely, employing the v-c induction method, which was perfectly legal of course but rather more dramatic than Haber liked to use in front of an observer from HEW; he was furious with Orr, in whom he had sensed growing resistance for the last five or six sessions. Once he had the man under, he put on a tape he had cut himself, of all the boring repetition of deepening trance and posthypnotic suggestion for rehypnotizing: "You are comfortable and relaxed now. You are sinking deeper into trance," and so on and so on. While it played he went back to his desk and sorted through papers with a calm, serious face, ignoring the Lelache. She kept still, knowing the hypnotic routine must not be interrupted; she was looking out the window at the view, the towers of the city.

At last Haber stopped the tape and put the trancap on Orr's head. "Now, while I'm hooking you up let's talk about what kind of dream you're going to dream, George. You feel like talking about that, don't you?"

Slow nod from the patient.

"Last time you were here we were talking about some things that worry you. You said you like your work, but you don't like riding the subway to work. You keep feeling crowded in on, you said—squeezed, pressed together. You feel as if you had no elbow room, as if you weren't free."

He paused, and the patient, who was always taciturn in hypnosis, at last responded merely: "Overpopulation."

"Mhm, that was the word you used. That's your word, your metaphor, for this feeling of unfreedom. Well, now, let's discuss that word. You know that back in the eighteenth century Malthus was pressing the panic button about population growth; and there was another fit of panic about it thirty, forty years ago. And sure enough population has gone up; but all the horrors they predicted just haven't come to pass. It's just not as bad as they said it would be. We all get by just fine here in America, and if our living standard has had to lower in some ways it's even higher in others than it was a generation ago. Now perhaps an excessive dread of overpopulation—overcrowding—reflects not an outward reality, but an inward state of mind. If you feel overcrowded when you're not, what does that mean? Maybe that you're afraid of human contact—of being close to people, of being touched. So you've found a kind of excuse for keeping reality at a distance." The EEG was running, and as he talked he made the connections to the Augmentor. "Now, George, we'll be talking a little longer and then when I say the key word 'Antwerp' you'll drop off to sleep; when you wake up you'll feel refreshed and alert. You won't recall what I'm saying now, but you will recall your dream. It'll be a vivid dream, vivid and pleasant, an effective dream. You'll dream about this thing that worries you, overpopulation: you'll have a dream where you find out that it isn't really that that worries you. People can't live alone, after all; to be put in solitary is the worst kind of confinement! We *need* people around us. To help us, to give help to, to compete with, to sharpen our wits against." And so on and so on. The lawyer's presence cramped his style badly; he had to put it all in abstract terms, instead of just telling Orr what to dream. Of course, he wasn't falsifying his method in order to deceive the observer; his method simply wasn't yet invariable. He varied it from session to session, seeking for the sure way to suggest the precise dream he wanted, and always coming up against the resistance that seemed to him sometimes to be the overliteralness of primary-process thinking, and sometimes to be a positive balkiness in Orr's mind. Whatever prevented it, the dream almost never came out the way Haber had intended; and this vague, abstract kind of suggestion might work as well as any. Perhaps it would rouse less unconscious resistance in Orr.

He gestured to the lawyer to come over and watch the

61

EEG screen, at which she had been peering from her corner, and went on: "You're going to have a dream in which you feel uncrowded, unsqueezed. You'll dream about all the elbow room there is in the world, all the freedom you have to move around." And at last he said, "Antwerp!"—and pointed to the EEG traces so that the Lelache would see the almost instantaneous change. "Watch the slowing down all across the graph," he murmured. "There's a high-voltage peak, see, there's another. . . . Sleep spindles. He's already going into the second stage of orthodox sleep, s-sleep, whichever term you've run into, the kind of sleep without vivid dreams that occurs in between the d-states all night. But I'm not letting him go on down into deep fourth-stage, since he's here to dream. I'm turning on the Augmentor. Keep your eye on those traces. Do you see?"

"Looks like he was waking up again," she murmured doubtfully.

"Right! But it's not waking. Look at him."

Orr lay supine, his head fallen back a little so that his short, fair beard jutted up; he was sound asleep, but there was a tension about his mouth; he sighed deeply.

"See his eyes move, under the lids? That's how they first caught this whole phenomenon of dreaming sleep, back in the 1930's; they called it rapid-eye-movement sleep, REM, for years. It's a hell of a lot more than that, though. It's a third state of being. His whole autonomic system is as fully mobilized as it might be in an exciting moment of waking life; but his muscle tone is nil, the large muscles are relaxed more deeply than in s-sleep. Cortical, subcortical, hippocampal, and midbrain areas all as active as in waking, whereas they're inactive in s-sleep. His respiration and blood pressure are up to waking levels or higher. Here, feel the pulse." He put her fingers against Orr's lax wrist. "Eighty or eighty-five, he's going. He's having a humdinger, whatever it is. . . ."

"You mean he's dreaming?" She looked awed.

"Right."

"Are all these reactions normal?"

"Absolutely. We all go through this performance every

night, four or five times, for at least ten minutes at a time. This is a quite normal d-state EEG on the screen. The only anomaly or peculiarity about it that you might be able to catch is an occasional high peaking right through the traces, a kind of brainstorm effect I've never seen in a d-state EEG before. Its pattern seems to resemble an effect that's been observed in electroencephalograms of men hard at work of a certain sort: creative or artistic work, painting, writing verse, even reading Shakespeare. What this brain is doing at those moments, I don't yet know. But the Augmentor gives me the opportunity to observe them systematically, and so eventually to analyze them out."

"There's no chance that the machine is causing this effect?"

"No." As a matter of fact, he had tried stimulating Orr's brain with a playback of one of these peak traces, but the dream resulting from that experiment had been incoherent, a mishmash of the previous dream, during which the Augmentor had recorded the peak, and the present one. No need to mention inconclusive experiments. "Now that he's well into this dream, in fact, I'll cut the Augmentor out. Watch, see if you can tell when I cut off the input." She couldn't. "He may produce a brainstorm for us anyhow; keep an eye on those traces. You may catch it first in the theta rhythm, there, from the hippocampus. It occurs in other brains, undoubtedly. Nothing's new. If I can find out *what* other brains, in what state, I may be able to specify much more exactly what this subject's trouble is; there may be a psychological or neurophysiological type to which he belongs. You see the research possibilities of the Augmentor? No effect on the patient except that of temporarily putting his brain into whichever of its own normal states the physician wants to observe. Look there!" She missed the peak, of course; EEG-reading on a moving screen took practice. "Blew his fuse. Still in the dream now. . . . He'll tell us about it presently." He could not go on talking. His mouth had gone dry. He felt it: the shift, the arrival, the change.

The woman felt it too. She looked frightened. Holding the heavy brass necklace up close to her throat like a talisman, she was staring in dismay, shock, terror, out the window at the view.

He had not expected that. He had thought that only he could be aware of the change.

But she had heard him tell Orr what to dream; she had stood beside the dreamer; she was there at the center, like him. And like him had turned to look out the window at the vanishing towers fade like a dream, leave not a wrack behind, the insubstantial miles of suburb dissolving like smoke on the wind, the city of Portland, which had had a population of a million people before the Plague Years but had only about a hundred thousand these days of the Recovery, a mess and jumble like all American cities, but unified by its hills and its misty, seven-bridged river, the old forty-story First National Bank building dominating the downtown skyline, and far beyond, above it all, the serene and pale mountains. . . .

She saw it happen. And he realized that he had never once thought that the HEW observer might see it happen. It hadn't been a possibility, he hadn't given it a thought. And this implied that he himself had not believed in the change, in what Orr's dreams did. Though he had felt it, seen it, with bewilderment, fear, and exultation, a dozen times now; though he had watched the horse become a mountain (if you can watch the overlap of one reality with another), though he had been testing, and using, the effective power of Orr's dreams for nearly a month now, yet he had not believed in what was happening.

This whole day, from his arrival at work on, he had not given one thought to the fact that, a week ago, he had not been the Director of the Oregon Oneirological Institute, because there had been no Institue. Ever since last Friday, there had been an Institute for the last eighteen months. And he had been its founder and director. And this being the way it was—for him, for everyone on the staff, and his colleagues at the Medical School, and the Government that funded it—he had accepted it totally, just as they did, as the only reality. He had suppressed his memory of the fact that, until last Friday, this had *not* been the way it was.

That had been Orr's most successful dream by far. It had begun in the old office across the river, under that damned mural photograph of Mount Hood, and had ended in this office . . . and he had been there, had seen the walls change around him, had known the world was being remade, and had forgotten it. He had forgotten it so completely that he had never even wondered if a stranger, a third person, might have the same experience.

What would it do to the woman? Would she understand, would she go mad, what would she do? Would she keep both memories, as he did, the true one and the new one, the old one and the true one?

She must not. She would interfere, bring in other observers, spoil the experiment completely, wreck his plans.

He would stop her at any cost. He turned to her, ready for violence, his hands clenched.

She was just standing there. Her brown skin had gone livid, her mouth was open. She was dazed. She could not believe what she had seen out that window. She could not and did not.

Haber's extreme physical tension relaxed a little. He was fairly sure, looking at her, that she was so confused and traumatized as to be harmless. But he must move quickly, all the same.

"He'll sleep for a while now," he said; his voice sounded almost normal, though hoarsened by the tightness of his throat muscles. He had no idea what he was going to say, but plunged ahead; anything to break the spell. "I'll let him have a short s-sleep period now. Not too long, or his dream recall will be poor. It's a nice view, isn't it? These easterly winds we've been having, they're godsend. In fall and winter I don't see the mountains for months at a go. But when the coluds clear off, there they are. It's a great place, Oregon. Most unspoiled state in the Union. Wasn't exploited much before the Crash. Portland was just beginning to get big in the late seventies. Are you a native Oregonian?"

After a minute she nodded groggily. The matter-of-fact tone of his voice, if nothing else, was getting through to her.

"I'm from New Jersey originally. It was terrible there when I was a kid, the environmental deterioration. The amount of tearing down and cleaning up the East Coast had to do after the Crash, and is still doing, is unbelievable. Out here, the real damage of overpopulation and environmental mismanagement hadn't yet been done, except in California. The Oregon ecosystem was still intact." It was dangerous, this talking right on the critical subject, but he could not think of anything else: he was as if compelled. His head was too full, holding the two sets of memories, two full systems of information: one of the real (no longer) world with a human population of nearly seven billion and increasing geometrically, and one of the real (now) world with a population of less than one billion and still not stabilized.

My God, he thought, what has Orr done?

Six billion people.

Where are they?

But the lawyer must not realize. Must not. "Ever been East, Miss Lelache?"

She looked at him vaguely and said, "No."

"Well, why bother. New York's doomed in any case, and Boston; and anyhow the future of this country is out here. This is the growing edge. This is where it's at, as they used to say when I as a kid! I wonder, by the way, if you know Dewey Furth, at the HEW office here."

"Yes," she said, still punch-drunk, but beginning to respond, to act as if nothing had happened. A spasm of relief went through Haber's body. He wanted to sit down suddenly, to breathe hard. The danger was past. She was rejecting the incredible experience. She was asking herself now, what's wrong with me? Why on earth did I look out the window expecting to see a city of three million? Am I having some sort of crazy spell?

Of course, Haber thought, a man who saw a miracle would reject his eyes' witness, if those with him saw nothing.

"It's stuffy in here," he said with a touch of solicitude in his voice, and went to the thermostat on the wall. "I keep it warm; old sleep-researcher's habit; body temperature falls during sleep, and you don't want a lot of subjects or patients with nose colds. But this electric heat's too efficient, it gets too warm, makes me feel groggy. . . . He should be waking soon." But he did not want Orr to recall his dream clearly, to recount it, to confirm the miracle. "I think I'll let him go a bit longer, I don't care about the recall on this dream, and he's right down in third-stage sleep now. Let him stay there while we finish talking. Was there anything else you wanted to ask about?"

"No. No, I don't think so." Her bangles clashed uncertainly. She blinked, trying to pull herself together. "If you'll send in the full description of your machine there, and its operation, and the current uses you're putting it to, and the results, all that, you know, to Mr. Furth's office, that should be the end of it. . . . Have you taken out a patent on the device?"

"Applied for one."

She nodded. "Might be worth while." She had wandered, clashing and clattering faintly, over toward the sleeping man, and now stood looking at him with an odd expression on her thin, brown face.

"You have a queer profession," she said abruptly. "Dreams; watching people's brains work; telling them what to dream. . . . I suppose you do a lot of your research at night?"

"Used to. The Augmentor may save us some of that; we'll be able to get sleep whenever we want, of the kind we want to study, using it. But a few years ago there was a period when I never went to bed before 6 A.M. for thirteen months." He laughed. "I boast about that now. My record. These days I let my staff carry most of the graveyard-shift load. Compensations of middle age!"

"Sleeping people are so remote," she said, still looking at Orr. "Where are they? . . ."

"Right here," Haber said, and tapped the EEG screen. "Right here, but out of communication. That's what strikes humans as uncanny about sleep. Its utter privacy. The sleeper turns his back on everyone. 'The mystery of the individual is strongest in sleep,' a writer in my field said. But of course a mystery is merely a problem we

67

haven't solved yet! . . . He's due to wake now. George . . . George . . . Wake up, George."

And he woke as he generally did, fast, shifting from one state to the other without groans, stares, and relapses. He sat up and looked first at Miss Lelache, then at Haber, who had just removed the trancap from his head. He got up, stretching a little, and went over to the window. He stood looking out.

There was a singular poise, almost a monumentality, in the stance of his slight figure: he was completely still, still as the center of something. Caught, neither Haber nor the woman spoke.

Orr turned around and looked at Haber.

"Where are they?" he said. "Where did they all go?"

Haber saw the woman's eyes open wide, saw the tension rise in her, and knew his peril. Talk, he must talk! "I'd judge from the EEG," he said, and heard his voice come out deep and warm, just as he wanted it, "that you had a highly charged dream just now, George. It was disagreeable; it was in fact very nearly a nightmare. The first 'bad' dream you've had here. Right?"

"I dreamed about the Plague," Orr said; and he shivered from head to foot, as if he were going to be sick.

Haber nodded. He sat down behind his desk. With his peculiar docility, his way of doing the habitual and acceptable thing, Orr came and sat down opposite in the big leather chair placed for interviewees and patients.

"You had a real hump to get over, and the getting over it wasn't easy. Right? This was the first time, George, that I've had you handle a real anxiety in a dream. This time, under my direction as suggested to you in hypnosis, you approached one of the deeper elements in your psychic malaise. The approach was not easy, or pleasant. In fact, that dream was a heller, wasn't it?"

"Do you remember the Plague Years?" Orr inquired, not aggressively, but with a tinge of something unusual in his voice: sarcasm? And he looked round at the Lelache, who had retired to her chair in the corner.

"Yes, I do. I was already a grown man when the first epidemic struck. I was twenty-two when that first an-

68

nouncement was made in Russia, that chemical pollutants in the atmosphere were combining to form virulent carcinogens. The next night they released the hospital statistics from Mexico City. Then they figured out the incubation period, and everybody began counting. Waiting. And there were the riots, and the fuck-ins, and the Doomsday Band, and the Vigilantes. And my parents died that year. My wife the next year. My two sisters and their children after that. Everyone I knew." Haber spread out his hands. "Yes, I remember those years," he said heavily. "When I must."

"They took care of the overpopulation problem, didn't they?" said Orr, and this time the edge was clear. "We really did it."

"Yes. They did. There is no overpopulation now. Was there any other solution, besides nuclear war? There is now no perpetual famine in South America, Africa, and Asia. When transport channels are fully restored, there won't be even the pockets of hunger that are still left. They say a third of humanity still goes to bed hungry at night; but in 1980 it was 92 per cent. There are no floods now in the Ganges caused by the piling up of corpses of people dead of starvation. There's no protein deprivation and rickets among the working-class children of Portland, Oregon. As there was—before the Crash."

"The Plague," Orr said.

Haber leaned forward across the big desk. "George. Tell me this. Is the world overpopulated?"

"No," the man said. Haber thought he was laughing, and drew back a little apprehensively; then he realized that it was tears that gave Orr's eyes that queer shine. He was near cracking. All the better. If he went to pieces, the lawyer would be still less inclined to believe anything he said that fitted with whatever she might recall.

"But half an hour ago, George, you were profoundly worried, anxious, because you believed that overpopulation was a present threat to civilization, to the whole Terran ecosystem. Now I don't expect that anxiety to be gone, far from it. But I believe its quality has changed, since your living through it in the dream. You are aware,

69

now, that it had no basis in reality. The anxiety still exists, but with this difference: you know now that it is irrational—that it conforms to an inward desire, rather than to outward reality. Now that's a beginning. A good beginning. A damn lot to have accomplished in one session, with one dream! Do you realize that? You've got a handle, now, to come at this whole thing with. You've got on top of something that's been on top of you, crushing you, making you feel pressed down and squeezed in. It's going to be a fairer fight from now on, because you're a freer man. Don't you feel that? Don't you feel, right now, already, just a little less crowded?"

Orr looked at him, then at the lawyer again. He said nothing.

There was a long pause.

"You look beat," Haber said, a verbal pat on the shoulder. He wanted to calm Orr down, to get him back into his normal self-effacing state, in which he would lack the courage to say anything about his dream powers in front of the third person; or else to get him to break right down, to behave with obvious abnormality. But he wouldn't do either. "If there wasn't an HEW observer lurking in the corner, I'd offer you a shot of whisky. But we'd better not turn a therapy session into a wing-ding, eh?"

"Don't you want to hear the dream?"

"If you want."

"I was burying them. In one of the big ditches . . . I did work in the Interment Corps, when I was sixteen, after my parents got it. . . . Only in the dream the people were all naked and looked like they'd died of starvation. Hills of them. I had to bury them all. I kept looking for you, but you weren't there."

"No," Haber said reassuringly, "I haven't figured in your dreams yet, George."

"Oh, yes. With Kennedy. And as a horse."

"Yes; very early in the therapy," Haber said, dismissing it. "This dream then did use some actual recall material from your experience—"

"No. I never buried anybody. Nobody died of the

Plague. There wasn't any Plague. It's all in my imagination. I dreamed it."

Damn the stupid little bastard! He had got out of control. Haber cocked his head and maintained a tolerant, noninterfering silence; it was all he could do, for a stronger move might make the lawyer suspicious.

"You said you remembered the Plague; but don't you also remember that there wasn't any Plague, that nobody died of pollutant cancer, that the population just kept on getting bigger and bigger? No? You don't remember that? What about you, Miss Lelache—do you remember it both ways?"

But at this Haber stood up: "Sorry, George, but I can't let Miss Lelache be drawn into this. She's not qualified. It would be improper for her to answer you. This is a psychiatric session. She's here to observe the Augmentor, and nothing further. I must insist on this."

Orr was quite white; the cheekbones stood out in his face. He sat staring up at Haber. He said nothing.

"We've got a problem here, and there's only one way to lick it, I'm afraid. Cut the Gordian knot. No offense, Miss Lelache, but as you can see, you're the problem. We're simply at a stage where our dialogue can't support a third member, even a nonparticipant. Best thing to do is just call it off. Right now. Start again tomorrow at four. O.K., George?"

Orr stood up, but didn't head for the door. "Did you ever happen to think, Dr. Haber," he said, quietly enough but stuttering a little, "that there, there might be other people who dream the way I do? That reality's being changed out from under us, replaced, renewed, all the time—only we don't know it? Only the dreamer knows it, and those who know his dream. If that's true, I guess we're lucky not knowing it. This is confusing enough."

Genial, noncommittal, reassuring, Haber talked him to the door, and out of it.

"You hit a crisis session," he said to the Lelache, shutting the door behind him. He wiped his forehead, let weariness and worry appear in his face and tone. "Whew! What a day to have an observer present!"

"It was extremely interesting," she said, and her bracelets chattered a little.

"He's not hopeless," Haber said. "A session like this one gives even me a pretty discouraging impression. But he has a chance, a real chance, of working out of this delusion pattern he's caught in, this terrific dread of dreaming. The trouble is, it's a complex pattern, and a not unintelligent mind caught in it; he's all too quick at weaving new nets to trap himself in. . . . If only he'd been sent for therapy ten years ago, when he was in his teens; but of course the Recovery had barely got underway ten years ago. Or even a year ago, before he started deteriorating his whole reality-orientation with drugs. But he tries, and keeps trying; and he may yet win through to a sound reality-adjustment."

"But he's not psychotic, you said," the Lelache remarked, a little dubiously.

"Correct. I said, disturbed. If he cracks, of course, he'll crack completely; probably in the catatonic schizophrenic line. A disturbed person isn't *less* liable to psychosis than a normal one." He could not talk any more, the words were drying up on his tongue, turning to dry shreds of nonsense. It seemed to him that he had been spewing out a deluge of meaningless speech for hours and now he had no more control over it at all. Fortunately Miss Lelache had had enough, too, evidently; she clashed, snapped, shook hands, left.

Haber went first to the tape recorder concealed in a wall panel near the couch, on which he recorded all therapy sessions: nonsignaling recorders were a special privilege of psychotherapists and the Office of Intelligence. He erased the record of the past hour.

He sat down in his chair behind the big oak desk, opened the bottom drawer, removed glass and bottle, and poured a hefty slug of bourbon. My God, there hadn't been any bourbon half an hour ago—not for twenty years! Grain had been far too precious, with seven billion mouths to feed, to go for spirits. There had been nothing but pseudobeer, or (for a doctor) absolute alcohol; that's what the bottle in his desk had been, half an hour ago.

He drank off half the shot in a gulp, then paused. He looked over at the window. After a while he got up and stood in front of the window looking out over the roofs and trees. One hundred thousand souls. Evening was beginning to dim the quiet river, but the mountains stood immense and clear, remote, in the level sunlight of the heights.

"To a better world!" Dr. Haber said, raising his glass to his creation, and finished his whisky in a lingering, savoring swallow.

6

It may remain for us to learn . . . that our task is
only beginning, and that there will never be given
to us even the ghost of any help, save the help of
unutterable and unthinkable Time. We may have
to learn that the infinite whirl of death and birth,
out of which we cannot escape, is of our own
creation, of our own seeking; — that the forces
integrating worlds are the errors of the Past; — that
the eternal sorrow is but the eternal hunger of
insatiable desire; — and that the burnt-out suns are
rekindled only by the inextinguishable passions of
vanished lives.

—Lafcadio Hearn, *Out of the East*

George Orr's apartment was on the top floor of an old
frame house a few blocks up the hill on Corbett Avenue, a
shabby part of town where most of the houses were
getting on for a century, or well beyond it. He had three
large rooms, a bathroom with a deep claw-foot tub, and a
view between roofs to the river, up and down which passed
ships, pleasure boats, logs, gulls, great turning flights of
pigeons.

He perfectly remembered his other flat, of course, the
one-room 8½ × 11 with the pullout stove and balloonbed
and co-op bathroom down the linoleum hall, on the
eighteenth floor of the Corbett Condominium tower, which
had never been built.

He got off the trolley at Whiteaker Street and walked up
the hill, and up the broad, dark stairs; he let himself in,
dropped his briefcase on the floor and his body on the
bed, and let go. He was terrified, anguished, exhausted,
bewildered. "I've got to do something, I've got to *do* some-

74

thing," he kept telling himself frantically, but he did not know what to do. He had never known what to do. He had always done what seemed to want doing, the next thing to be done, without asking questions, without forcing himself, without worrying about it. But that sureness of foot had deserted him when he began taking drugs, and by now he was quite astray. He must act, he had to *act*. He must refuse to let Haber use him any longer as a tool. He must take his destiny in his own hands.

He spread out his hands and looked at them, then sank his face into them; it was wet with tears. Oh hell, hell, he thought bitterly, what kind of man am I? Tears in my beard? No wonder Haber uses me. How could he help it? I haven't any strength, I haven't any character, I'm a born tool. I haven't any destiny. All I have is dreams. And now other people run them.

I must get away from Haber, he thought, trying to be firm and decisive, but even as he thought it he knew he wouldn't. Haber had him hooked, and with more than one hook.

A dream configuration so unusual, indeed unique, Haber had said, was invaluable to research: Orr's contribution to human knowledge was going to prove immense. Orr believed that Haber meant this and knew what he was talking about. The scientific aspect of it all was in fact the only hopeful one, to his mind; it seemed to him that perhaps science might wring some good out of his peculiar and terrible gift, put it to some good ends, compensating a little for the enormous harm it had done.

The murder of six billion nonexistent people.

Orr's head ached fit to split. He ran cold water in the deep, cracked washbasin, and dunked his whole face in for half a minute at a time, coming up red, blind, and wet as a newborn baby.

Haber had a moral line on him, then, but where he really had him caught was on the legal hook. If Orr quit Voluntary Therapy, he became liable to prosecution for obtaining drugs illegally and would be sent to jail or the nut hatch. No way out there. And if he didn't quit, but merely cut sessions and failed to cooperate, Haber had an

75

effective instrument of coercion: the dream-suppressing drugs, which Orr could obtain only on his prescription. He was more uneasy than ever at the idea of dreaming spontaneously, without control, now. In the state he was in, and having been conditioned to dream effectively every time in the laboratory, he did not like to think what might happen if he dreamed effectively without the rational restraints imposed by hypnosis. It would be a nightmare, a worse nightmare than the one he had just had in Haber's office; of that he was sure, and he dared not let it happen. He must take the dream suppressants. That was the one thing he knew he must do, the thing that must be done. But he could do it only so long as Haber let him, and therefore he must cooperate with Haber. He was caught. Rat in a trap. Running a maze for the mad scientist, and no way out. No way, no way.

Be he's not a mad scientist, Orr thought dully, he's a pretty sane one, or he was. It's the chance of power that my dreams give him that twists him around. He keeps acting a part, and this gives him such an awfully big part to play. So that now he's using even his science as a means, not an end. . . . But his ends are good, aren't they? He wants to improve life for humanity. Is that wrong?

His head was aching again. He was underwater when the telephone rang. He hastily tried to rub his face and hair dry, and returned to the dark bedroom, groping. "Hello, Orr here."

"This is Heather Lelache," said a soft, suspicious alto.

An irrelevant and poignant sensation of pleasure rose in him, like a tree that grew up and flowered all in one moment with its roots in his loins and its flowers in his mind. "Hello," he said again.

"Do you want to meet me some time to talk about this?"

"Yes. Certainly."

"Well. I don't want you thinking that there's any case to be made using that machine thing, the Augmentor. That seems to be perfectly in line. It's had extensive laboratory trial, and he's had all the proper checks and gone through the proper channels, and now it's registered with HEW.

He's a real pro, of course. I didn't realize who he was when you first talked to me. A man doesn't get to that sort of position unless he's awfully good."

"What position?"

"Well. The directorship of a Government-sponsored research institute!"

He liked the way she began her fierce, scornful sentences so often with a weak, conciliatory "well." She cut the ground out from under them before they ever got going, let them hang unsupported in the void. She had courage, great courage.

"Oh, yes, I see," he said vaguely. Dr. Haber had got his directorship the day after Orr had got his cabin. The cabin dream had been during the one all-night session they had had; they never tried another. Hypnotic suggestion of dream content was insufficient to a night's dreaming, and at 3 A.M. Haber had at last given up and, hooking Orr to the Augmentor, had fed him deep-sleep patterns the rest of the night, so that they could both relax. But the next afternoon they had had a session, and the dream Orr had dreamed during it had been so long, so confused and complicated, that he had never been altogether sure of what he had changed, what good works Haber had been accomplishing that time. He had gone to sleep in the old office and had wakened in the O.O.I. office: Haber had got himself a promotion. But there had been more to it than that—the weather was a little less rainy, it seemed, since that dream; perhaps other things had changed. He was not sure. He had protested against doing so much effective dreaming in so short a time. Haber had at once agreed not to push him so fast, and had let him go without a session for five days. Haber was, after all, a benevolent man. And besides, he didn't want to kill the goose that laid the golden eggs.

The goose. Precisely. That describes me perfectly, Orr thought. A damned white vapid stupid goose. He had lost a bit of what Miss Lelache was saying. "I'm sorry," he said, "I missed something. I'm kind of thick-headed just now, I think."

"Are you all right?"

"Yes, fine. Just sort of tired."

"You had an upsetting dream, about the Plague, didn't you. You looked awful after it. Do these sessions leave you this way every time?"

"No, not always. This was a bad one. I guess you could see that. Were you arranging for us to meet?"

"Yes. Monday for lunch, I said. You work downtown, don't you, at Bradford Industries?"

To his mild wonder he realized that he did. The great water projects of Bonneville-Umatilla did not exist, to bring water to the giant cities of John Day and French Glen, which did not exist. There were no big cities in Oregon, except Portland. He was not a draftsman for the District, but for a private tools firm downtown; he worked in the Stark Street office. Of course. "Yes," he said. "I'm off from one to two. We could meet at Dave's, on Ankeny."

"One to two is fine. So's Dave's. I'll see you there Monday."

"Wait," he said. "Listen. Will you—would you mind telling me what Dr. Haber said, I mean, what he told me to dream when I was hypnotized? You heard all that, didn't you?"

"Yes, but I couldn't do that, I'd be interfering in his treatment. If he wanted you to know he'd tell you. It would be unethical, I can't."

"I guess that's right."

"Yes. I'm sorry. Monday, then?"

"Goodby," he said, suddenly overwhelmed with depression and foreboding, and put the receiver back without hearing her say goodby. She couldn't help him. She was courageous and strong, but not that strong. Perhaps she had seen or sensed the change, but she had put it away from her, refused it. Why not? It was a heavy load to bear, that double memory, and she had no reason to undertake it, no motive for believing even for a moment a driveling psycho who claimed that his dreams came true.

Tomorrow was Saturday. A long session with Haber, four o'clock until six or longer. No way out.

It was time to eat, but Orr wasn't hungry. He had not

turned on the lights in his high, twilit bedroom, or in the living room which he had never got around to furnishing in the three years he'd lived here. He wandered in there now. The windows looked out on lights and the river, the air smelled of dust and early spring. There was a woodframe fireplace, an old upright piano with eight ivories missing, a pile of carpeting mill ends by the hearth, and a decrepit Japanese bamboo table ten inches high. Darkness lay softly on the bare pine floor, unpolished, unswept.

George Orr lay down in that mild darkness, full length, face down, the small of the dusty wooden floor in his nostrils, the hardness of it upholding his body. He lay still, not asleep; somewhere else than sleep, farther on, father out, a place where there are no dreams. It was not the first time he had been there.

When he got up, it was to take a chlorpromazine tablet and go to bed. Haber had tried him with phenothiazines this week; they seemed to work well, to let him enter the d-state at need but to weaken the intensity of the dreams so that they never rose to the effective level. That was fine, but Haber said that the effect would lessen, just as with all the other drugs, until there was no effect at all. Nothing will keep a man from dreaming, he had said, but death.

This night, at least, he slept deep, and if he dreamed the dreams were fleeting, without weight. He didn't wake until nearly noon on Saturday. He went to his refrigerator and look in it; he stood contemplating it a while. There was more food in it than he had ever seen in a private refrigerator in his life. In his other life. The one lived among seven billion others, where the food, such as it was, was never enough. Where an egg was the luxury of the month —"Today we ovulate!" his halfwife had used to say when she bought their egg ration. . . . Curious, in this life they hadn't had a trial marriage, he and Donna. There was no such thing, legally speaking, in the post-Plague years. There was full marriage only. In Utah, since the birth rate was still lower than the death rate, they were even trying to reinstitute polygamous marriage, for religious and patriotic reasons. But he and Donna hadn't had any kind of marriage this time, they had just lived together. But still it hadn't lasted. His attention returned to the food in the refrigerator.

He was not the thin, sharp-boned man he had been in the world of the seven billion; he was quite solid, in fact. But he ate a starving man's meal, an enormous meal—hard-boiled eggs, buttered toast, anchovies, jerky, celery, cheese, walnuts, a piece of cold halibut spread with mayonnaise, lettuce, pickled beets, chocolate cookies—anything he found on his shelves. After this orgy he felt physically a great deal better. He thought of something, as he drank some genuine nonersatz coffee, that actually made him grin. He thought: In *that* life, yesterday, I dreamed an effective dream, which obliterated six billion lives and changed the entire history of humankind for the past quarter century. But in *this* life, which I then created, I did *not* dream an effective dream. I was in Haber's office, all right, and I dreamed; but it didn't change anything. It's been this way all along, and I merely had a bad dream about the Plague Years. There's nothing wrong with me; I don't need therapy.

He had never looked at it this way before, and it amused him enough that he grinned, but not particularly happily.

He knew he would dream again.

It was already past two. He washed up, found his raincoat (real cotton, a luxury in the other life), and set off on foot to the Institute, a couple of miles' walk, up past the Medical School and then farther up, into Washington Park. He could have got there by the trolleys, of course, but they were sporadic and roundabout, and anyhow there was no rush. It was pleasant, passing through the warm March rain, the unbustling streets; the trees were leafing out, the chestnuts ready to light their candles.

The Crash, the carcinomic plague which had reduced human population by five billion in five years, and another billion in the next ten, had shaken the civilizations of the world to their roots and yet left them, in the end, intact. If had not changed anything radically: only quantitatively.

The air was still profoundly and irremediably polluted: that pollution predated the Crash by decades, indeed was its direct cause. It didn't harm anybody much now, except the newborn. The Plague, in its leukemoid variety, still selectively, thoughtfully as it were, picked off one out of four babies born and killed it within six months. Those who survived were virtually cancer-resistant. But there are other griefs.

No factories spewed smoke, down by the river. No cars ran fouling the air with exhaust; what few there were, were steamers or battery-powered.

There were no songbirds any more, either.

The effects of the Plague were visible in everything, it was itself still endemic, and yet it hadn't prevented war from breaking out. In fact the fighting in the Near East was more savage than it had been in the more crowded world. The U.S. was heavily committed to the Israeli-Egyptian side in weapons, munitions, planes, and "military advisers" by the regiment. China was in equally deep on the Iraq-Iran side, though she hadn't yet sent in Chinese soldiers, only Tibetans, North Koreans, Vietnamese, and Mongolians. Russia and India were holding uneasily aloof; but now that Afghanistan and Brazil were going in with the Iranians, Pakistan might jump in on the Isragypt side. India would then panic and line up with China, which might scare the USSR enough to push her in on the U.S. side. This gave a line-up of twelve Nuclear Powers in all, six to a side. So went the speculations. Meanwhile Jerusalem was rubble, and in Saudi Arabia and Iraq the civilian population was living in burrows in the ground while tanks and planes sprayed fire in the air and cholera in the water, and babies crawled out of the burrows blinded by napalm.

They were still massacring whites in Johannesburg, Orr noticed on a headline at a corner newspaper stand. Years now since the Uprising, and there were still whites to massacre in South Africa! People are tough. . . .

The rain fell warm, polluted, gentle on his bare head as he climbed the gray hills of Portland.

In the office with the great corner window that looked out into the rain, he said, "Please, stop using my dreams to improve things, Dr. Haber. It won't work. It's wrong. I want to be *cured*."

"That's the one essential prerequisite to your cure, George! *Wanting* it."

"You're not answering me."

But the big man was like an onion, slip off layer after layer of personality, belief, response, infinite layers, no end to them, no center to him. Nowhere that he ever stopped, had to stop, had to say Here I stay! No being, only layers.

"You're using my effective dreams to change the world. You won't admit to me that you're doing it. Why not?"

"George, you must realize that you ask questions which from your point of view may seem reasonable, but which from my point of view are literally unanswerable. We don't see reality the same way."

"Near enough the same to be able to talk."

"Yes. Fortunately. But not always to be able to ask and answer. Not yet."

"I can answer your questions, and I do. . . . But anyway: look. You can't go on changing things, trying to run things."

"You speak as if that were some kind of general moral imperative." He looked at Orr with his genial, reflective smile, stroking his beard. "But in fact, isn't that man's very purpose on earth—to do things, change things, run things, make a better world?"

"No!"

"What is his purpose, then?"

"I don't know. Things don't have purposes, as if the universe were a machine, where every part has a useful function. What's the function of a galaxy? I don't know if our life has a purpose and I don't see that it matters. What does matter is that we're a part. Like a thread in a cloth or a grass-blade in a field. It *is* and we *are*. What we do is like wind blowing on the grass."

There was a slight pause, and when Haber answered his tone was no longer genial, reassuring, or encouraging. It was quite neutral and verged, just detectably, on contempt.

"You're of a peculiarly passive outlook for a man brought up in the Judaeo-Christian-Rationalist West. A sort of natural Buddhist. Have you ever studied the Eastern mysticisms, George?" The last question, with its obvious answer, was an open sneer.

"No. I don't know anything about them. I do know that it's wrong to force the pattern of things. It won't do. It's been our mistake for a hundred years. Don't you—don't you see what happened yesterday?"

The opaque, dark eyes met his, straight on.

"What happened yesterday, George?"

No way. No way out.

Haber was using sodium pentothal on him now, to lower his resistance to hypnotic procedures. He submitted to the shot, watching the needle slip with only a moment of pain into the vein of his arm. This was the way he had to go; he had no choice. He had never had any choice. He was only a dreamer.

Haber went off somewhere to run something while the drug took effect; but he was back promptly in fifteen minutes, gusty, jovial, and indifferent. "All right! Let's get on with it, George!"

Orr knew, with dreary clarity, what he would get on with today: the war. The papers were full of it, even Orr's news-resistant mind had been full of it, coming here. The growing war in the Near East. Haber would end it. And no doubt the killings in Africa. For Haber was a benevolent man. He wanted to make the world better for humanity.

The end justifies the means. But what if there never is an end? All we have is means. Orr lay back on the couch and shut his eyes. The hand touched his throat. "You will enter the hypnotic state now, George," said Haber's deep voice. "You are. . . ."

dark.

In the dark.

Not quite night yet: late twilight on the fields. Clumps of trees looked black and moist. The road he was walking on picked up the faint, last light from the sky; it ran long and straight, an old country highway, cracked blacktop. A goose was walking ahead of him, about fifteen feet in advance and visible only as a white, bobbing blur. Now and then it hissed a little.

The stars were coming out, white as daisies. A big one was blooming just to the right of the road, low over the dark country, tremulously white. When he looked up at it again it had already become larger and brighter. *It's enhuging,* he thought. It seemed to grow reddish as it brightened. It enreddenhuged. The eyes swam. Small blue-green streaks zipped about it zigzagging Brownian round-ianroundian. A vast and creamy halo pulsated about big star and tiny zips, fainter, clearer, pulsing. *Oh no no no!* he said as the big star brightened hugendly BURST blinding. He fell to the ground, covering his head with his arms as the sky burst into streaks of bright death, but could not turn onto his face, must behold and witness. The ground swung up and down, great trembling wrinkles passing through the skin of Earth. "Let be, let be!" he screamed aloud with his face against the sky, and woke on the leather couch.

He sat up, and put his face in his sweaty, shaking hands.

Presently he felt Haber's hand heavy on his shoulder. "Bad time again? Damn, I thought I'd let you off easy. Told you to have a dream about peace."

"I did."

"But it was disturbing to you?"

"I was watching a battle in space."

"Watching it? From where?"

"Earth." He recounted the dream briefly, omitting the goose. "I don't know whether they got one of ours or we got one of theirs."

Haber laughed. "I wish we *could* see what goes on out there! We'd feel more involved. But of course those encounters take place at speeds and distances that human vision simply isn't equipped to keep up with. Your version's a lot more picturesque than the actuality, no doubt. Sounds like a good science-fiction movie from the seventies. Used to go to those when I was a kid. . . . But why do you think you dreamed up a battle scene when the suggestion was peace?"

"Just peace? Dream about peace—that's all you said?"

Haber did not answer at once. He occupied himself with the controls of the Augmentor.

"O.K.," he said at last. "This once, experimentally, let's let you compare the suggestion with the dream. Perhaps we'll find out why it came out negative. I said—no, let's run the tape." He went over to a panel in the wall.

"You tape the whole session?"

"Sure. Standard psychiatric practice. Didn't you know?"

How could I know if it's hidden, makes no noise signal, and you didn't tell me, Orr thought; but he said nothing. Maybe it was standard practice, maybe it was Haber's personal arrogance; but in either case he couldn't do much about it.

"Here we are, it ought to be about here. The hypnotic state now, George. You are—Here! Don't go under, George!" The tape hissed. Orr shook his head and blinked. The last fragments of sentences had been Haber's voice on the tape, of course; and he was still full of the hypnosis-inducing drug.

"I'll have to skip a bit. All right." Now it was his voice on the tape again, saying, "—peace. No more mass killing of humans by other humans. No fighting in Iran and Arabia and Israel. No more genocides in Africa. No stockpiles of nuclear and biological weapons, ready to use against other nations. No more research on ways and means of killing people. A world at peace with itself. Peace as a universal life-style on Earth. You will dream of that world at peace with itself. Now you're going to sleep. When I say—" He stopped the tape abruptly, lest he put Orr to sleep with the key word.

Orr rubbed his forehead. "Well," he said, "I followed instructions."

"Hardly. To dream of a battle in cislunar space—" Haber stopped as abruptly as the tape.

"Cislunar," Orr said, feeling a little sorry for Haber. "We weren't using that word, when I went to sleep. How are things in Isragypt?"

The made-up word from the old reality had a curiously shocking effect, spoken in this reality: like surrealism, it seemed to make sense and didn't, or seemed not to make sense and did.

85

Haber walked up and down the long, handsome room. Once he passed his hand over his red-brown, curly beard. The gesture was a calculated one and familiar to Orr, but when he spoke Orr felt that he was seeking and choosing his words carefully, not trusting, for once, to his inexhaustible fund of improvisation. "It's curious that you used the Defense of Earth as a symbol or metaphor of peace, of the end of warfare. Yet it's not unfitting. Only very subtle. Dreams are endlessly subtle. Endlessly. For in fact it *was* that threat, that immediate peril of invasion by noncommunicating, reasonlessly hostile aliens, which forced us to stop fighting among ourselves, to turn our aggressive-defensive energies outward, to extend the territorial drive to include all humanity, to combine our weapons against a common foe. If the Aliens hadn't struck, who knows? We might, actually, still be fighting in the Near East."

"Out of the frying pan into the fire," Orr said. "Don't you see, Dr. Haber, that that's all you'll ever get from me? Look, it's not that I want to block you, to frustrate your plans. Ending the war was a good idea, I agree with it totally. I even voted Isolationist last election because Harris promised to pull us out of the Near East. But I guess I can't, or my subconscious can't, even imagine a warless world. The best it can do is substitute one kind of war for another. You said, no killing of humans by other humans. So I dreamed up the Aliens. Your own ideas are sane and rational, but this is my unconscious you're trying to use, not my rational mind. Maybe rationally I could conceive of the human species not trying to kill each other off by nations, in fact rationally it's easier to conceive of than the motives of war. But you're handling something outside reason. You're trying to reach progressive, humanitarian goals with a tool that isn't suited to the job. Who has humanitarian dreams?"

Haber said nothing, and showed no reaction, so Orr went on.

"Or maybe it's not just my unconscious, irrational mind, maybe it's my total self, my whole being, that just isn't right for the job. I'm too defeatist, or passive, as you

86

said, maybe. I don't have enough desires. Maybe that has something to do with my having this—this capacity to dream effectively; but if it doesn't, there might be others who can do it, people with minds more like your own, that you could work with better. You could test for it; I can't be the only one; maybe I just happened to become aware of it. But I don't *want* to do it. I want to get off the hook. I can't take it. I mean, look: all right, the war's been over in the Near East for six years, fine, but now there are the Aliens, up on the Moon. What if they land? What kind of monsters have you dredged up out of my unconscious mind, in the name of peace? I don't even know!"

"Nobody knows what the Aliens look like, George," Haber said, in a reasonable, reassuring tone. "We all have our bad dreams about 'em, God knows! But as you said, it's been over six years now since their first landing on the Moon, and they still haven't made it to Earth. By now, our missile defense systems are completely efficient. There's no reason to think they'll break through now, if they haven't yet. The danger period was during those first few months, before the Defense was mobilized on an international cooperative basis."

Orr sat a while, shoulders slumped. He wanted to yell at Haber, "Liar! Why do you lie to me?" But the impulse was not a deep one. It led nowhere. For all he knew, Haber was incapable of sincerity because he was lying to himself. He might be compartmenting his mind into two hermetic halves, in one of which he knew that Orr's dreams changed reality, and employed them for that purpose; in the other of which he knew that he was using hypnotherapy and dream abreaction to treat a schizoid patient who believed that his dreams changed reality.

That Haber could have thus got out of communication with himself was rather hard for Orr to conceive; his own mind was so resistant to such divisions that he was slow to recognize them in others. But he had learned that they existed. He had grown up in a country run by politicians who sent the pilots to man the bombers to kill the babies to make the world safe for children to grow up in.

But that was in the old world, now. Not in the brave new one.

"I am cracking," he said. "You must see that. You're a psychiatrist. Don't you see that I'm going to pieces? Aliens from outer space attacking Earth! Look: if you ask me to dream again, what will you get? Maybe a totally insane world, the product of an insane mind. Monsters, ghosts, witches, dragons, transformations—all the stuff we carry around in us, all the horrors of childhood, the night fears, the nightmares. How can you keep all that from getting loose? I can't stop it. I'm not in control!"

"Don't worry about control! Freedom is what you're working toward," Haber said gustily. "Freedom! Your unconscious mind is not a sink of horror and depravity. That's a Victorian notion, and a terrifically destructive one. It crippled most of the best minds of the nineteenth century, and hamstrung psychology all through the first half of the twentieth. Don't be afraid of your unconscious mind! It's not a black pit of nightmares. Nothing of the kind! It is the wellspring of health, imagination, creativity. What we call 'evil' is produced by civilization, its constraints and repressions, deforming the spontaneous, free self-expression of the personality. The aim of psychotherapy is precisely this, to remove those groundless fears and nightmares, to bring up what's unconscious into the light of rational consciousness, examine it objectively, and find that there is *nothing to fear.*"

"But there is," Orr said very softly.

Haber let him go at last. He came out into the spring twilight, and stood a minute on the steps of the Institute with his hands in his pockets, looking at the streetlights in the city below, so blurred by mist and dusk that they seemed to wink and move like the tiny, silvery shapes of tropical fish in a dark aquarium. A cable car was clanking up the steep hill toward its turnaround here at the top of Washington Park, in front of the Institute. He went out into the street and climbed aboard the car while it was turning. His walk was evasive and yet aimless. He moved like a sleepwalker, like one impelled.

7

Daydream, which is to thought as the nebula is to
the star, borders on sleep, and is concerned with it
as its frontier. An atmosphere inhabited by living
transparencies: there's a beginning of the unknown. But beyond it the Possible opens out,
immense. Other beings, other facts, are there. No
supernaturalism, only the occult continuation of
infinite nature. . . . Sleep is in contact with the
Possible, which we also call the improbable. The
world of the night is a world. Night, as night, is a
universe. . . . The dark things of the unknown
world become neighbors of man, whether by true
communication or by a visionary enlargement of
the distances of the abyss . . . and the sleeper, not
quite seeing, not quite unconscious, glimpses the
strange animalities, weird vegetations, terrible or
radiant pallors, ghosts, masks, figures, hydras, con-
fusions, moonless moonlights, obscure unmakings
of miracle, growths and vanishings within a murky
depth, shapes floating in shadow, the whole
mystery which we call Dreaming, and which is
nothing other than the approach of an invisible
reality. The dream is the aquarium of Night.
                    —V. Hugo, *Travailleurs de la Mer*

At 2:10 P.M. on March 30, Heather Lelache was seen
leaving Dave's Fine Foods on Ankeny Street and proceeding southward on Fourth Avenue, carrying a large
black handbag with brass catch, wearing a red vinyl rain-
cloak. Look out for this woman. She is dangerous.

It wasn't that she cared one way or the other about
seeing that poor damned psycho, but shit, she hated to
look foolish in front of waiters. Holding a table for half an
hour right in the middle of the lunchtime crowd—"I'm

waiting for somebody."—"I'm sorry, I'm waiting for somebody."—and so nobody comes and nobody comes, and so finally she had to order and shove the stuff down in a big rush, and so now she'd have heartburn. On top of pique, umbrage, and ennui. Oh, the French diseases of the soul.

She turned left on Morrison, and then suddenly stopped. What was she doing over here? This wasn't the way to Forman, Esserbeck, and Rutti. Hastily she returned north several blocks, crossed Ankeny, came to Burnside, and stopped again. What the hell was she doing?

Going to the converted parking structure at 209 S.W. Burnside. What converted parking structure? Her office was in the Pendleton Building, Portland's first post-Crash office building, on Morrison. Fifteen stories, neo-Inca decor. What converted parking structure, who the hell worked in a converted parking structure?

She went on down Burnside and looked. Sure enough, there it was. There were Condemned signs all over it.

Her office was up there on the third level.

As she stood down on the sidewalk staring up at the disused building with its queer, slightly skewed floors and narrow window slits, she felt very strange indeed. What had *happened* last Friday at that psychiatric session?

She had to see that little bastard again. Mr. Either Orr. So he stood her up for lunch, so what, she still had some questions to ask him. She strode south, click clack, pincers snapping, to the Pendleton Building, and called him from her office. First at Bradford Industries (no, Mr. Orr didn't come in today, no, he hasn't called in), then at his residence (ring. ring. ring.).

She should call Dr. Haber again, maybe. But he was such a big shot, running the Palace of Dreams up there in the park. And anyhow what was she thinking of: Haber wasn't supposed to know she had any connection with Orr. Liar builds pitfall, falls in it. Spider stuck in own web.

That night Orr did not answer his telephone at seven, nine, or eleven. He was not at work Tuesday morning, nor at two o'clock Tuesday afternoon. At four-thirty Tuesday afternoon Heather Lelache left the offices of Forman,

Esserbeck, and Rutti, and took the trolley out to Whiteaker Street, walked up the hill to Corbett Avenue, found the house, rang the bell: one of six infinitely thumbed bell pushes in a grubby little row on the peeling frame of the cut-glass-paneled door of a house that had been somebody's pride and joy in 1905 or 1892, and that had come on hard times since but was proceeding toward ruin with composure and a certain dirty magnificence. No answer when she rang Orr's bell. She rang M. Ahrens Manager. Twice. Manager came, was uncooperative at first. But one thing the Black Widow was good at was the intimidation of lesser insects. Manager took her upstairs and tried Orr's door. It opened. He hadn't locked it.

She stepped back. All at once she thought there might be death inside. And it was not her place.

Manager, unconcerned with private property, barged on in, and she followed, reluctant.

The big, old, bare rooms were shadowy and unoccupied. It seemed silly to have thought of death. Orr did not own much; there was no bachelor slop and disarray, no bachelor prim tidiness either. There was little impress of his personality on the rooms, yet she saw him living there, a quiet man living quietly. There was a glass of water on the table in the bedroom, with a spray of white heather in it. The water had evaporated down about a quarter inch.

"I dono where he's gone to," Manager said crossly, and looked at her for help. "You think he hanaccident? Something?" Manager wore the fringed buckskin coat, the Cody mane, the Aquarius emblem necklace of his youth: he apparently had not changed his clothes for thirty years. He had an accusing Dylan whine. He even smelled of marijuana. Old hippies never die.

Heather looked at him kindly, for his smell reminded her of her mother. She said, "Maybe he went to the place he has over on the Coast. The thing is, he's not well, you know, he's on Government Therapy. He'll get in trouble if he stays away. Do you know where that cabin is, or if he has a phone there?"

"I dono."

"Can I use your phone?"

"Use his," said Manager, shrugging.

She called up a friend in Oregon State Parks and got him to look up the thirty-four Siuslaw National Forest cabins which had been lotteried off and give her their location. Manager hung around to listen in, and when she was done said, "Friends in high places, huh?"

"It helps," the Black Widow answered, sibilant.

"Hope you dig George up. I like that cat. He borrows my Pharm Card," Manager said and all at once gave a great snort of laughter which was gone at once. Heather left him leaning morose against the peeling frame of the front door, he and the old house lending each other mutual support.

Heather took the trolley back downtown, rented a Ford Steamer at Hertz, and took off on 99-W. She was enjoying herself. The Black Widow pursues her prey. Why hadn't she been a detective instead of a goddam stupid third-class civil rights lawyer? She hated the law. It took an agressive, assertive personality. She didn't have it. She had a sneaky, sly, shy, squamous personality. She had French diseases of the soul.

The little car was soon free of the city, for the smear of suburbia that had once lain along the western highways for miles was gone. During the Plague Years of the eighties, when in some areas not one person in twenty remained alive, the suburbs were not a good place to be. Miles from the supermart, no gas for the car, and all the split-level ranch homes around you full of the dead. No help, no food. Packs of huge status-symbol dogs—Afghans, Alsatians, Great Danes—running wild across the lawns ragged with burdock and plantain. Picture window cracked. Who'll come and mend the broken glass? People had huddled back into the old core of the city; and once the suburbs had been looted, they burned. Like Moscow in 1812, acts of God or vandalism: they were no longer wanted, and they burned. Fireweed, from which bees make the finest honey of all, grew acre after acre over the sites of Kensington Homes West, Sylvan Oak Manor Estates, and Valley Vista Park.

The sun was setting when she crossed the Tualatin

92

River, still as silk between steep wooded banks. After a while the moon came up, near full, yellow to her left as the road went south. It worried her, looking over her shoulder on curves. It was no longer pleasant to exchange glances with the moon. It symbolized neither the Unattainable, as it had for thousands of years, nor the Attained, as it had for a few decades, but the Lost. A stolen coin, the muzzle of one's gun turned against one, a round hole in the fabric of the sky. The Aliens held the moon. Their first act of aggression—the first notice humanity had of their presence in the solar system—was the attack on the Lunar Base, the horrible murder by asphyxiation of the forty men in the bubble-dome. And at the same time, the same day, they had destroyed the Russian space platform, the queer beautiful thing like a big thistledown seed that had orbited Earth, and from which the Russians were going to step off to Mars. Only ten years after the remission of the Plague, the shattered civilization of mankind had come back up like a phoenix, into orbit, to the Moon, to Mars: and had met this. Shapeless, speechless, reasonless brutality. The stupid hatred of the universe.

Roads were not kept up the way they were when the Highway was king; there were rough bits and pot-holes. But Heather frequently got up to the speed limit (45 mph) as she drove through the broad, moonlit-twilit valley, crossing the Yamhill River four times or was it five, passing through Dundee and Grand Ronde, one a live village and the other deserted, as dead as Karnak, and coming at last into the hills, into the forests. Van Duzer Forest Corridor, ancient wooden road sign: land preserved long ago from the logging companies. Not quite all the forests of America had gone for grocery bags, split-levels, and Dick Tracy on Sunday morning. A few remained. A turnoff to the right: Siuslaw National Forest. And no goddam Tree Farm either, all stumps and sick seedlings, but virgin forest. Great hemlocks blackened the moonlit sky.

The sign she looked for was almost invisible in the branched and ferny dark that swallowed the pallid headlights. She turned again, and bumped slowly down ruts and over humps for a mile or so until she saw the first cabin, moonlight on a shingled roof. It was a little past eight o'clock.

The cabins were on lots, thirty or forty feet between them; few trees had been sacrificed, but the undergrowth had been cleared, and once she saw the pattern she could see the little roofs catching moonlight, and across the creek a facing set. Only one window was lighted, of them all. A Tuesday night in early spring: not many vacationers. When she opened the car door she was startled by the loudness of the creek, a hearty and unceasing roar. Eternal and uncompromising praise! She got to the lighted cabin, stumbling only twice in the dark, and looked at the car parked by it: a Hertz batcar. Surely. But what if it wasn't? It could be a stranger. Oh well, shit, they wouldn't eat her, would they. She knocked.

After a while, swearing silently, she knocked again.

The stream shouted loudly, the forest held very still.

Orr opened the door. His hair hung in locks and snarls, his eyes were bloodshot, his lips dry. He stared at her blinking. He looked degraded and undone. She was terrified of him. "Are you ill?" she said sharply.

"No, I . . . Come in. . . ."

She had to come in. There was a poker for the Franklin stove: she could defend herself with that. Of course, he could attack her with it, if he got it first.

Oh for Christsake she was as big as he was almost, and in lots better shape. Coward coward. "Are you high?"

"No, I . . ."

"You what? What's wrong with you?"

"I can't sleep."

The tiny cabin smelt wonderfully of woodsmoke and fresh wood. Its furniture was the Franklin stove with a two-plate cooker top, a box full of alder branches, a cabinet, a table, a chair, an army cot. "Sit down," Heather said. "You look terrible. Do you need a drink, or a doctor? I have some brandy in the car. You'd better come with me and we'll find a doctor in Lincoln City."

"I'm all right. It's just mumble mumble get sleepy."

"You said you couldn't sleep."

94

He looked at her with red, bleary eyes. "Can't let myself. Afraid to."

"Oh Christ. How long has this been going on?"

"Mumble mumble Sunday."

"You haven't slept since Sunday?"

"Saturday?" he said enquiringly.

"Did you take anything? Pep pills?"

He shook his head. "I did fall asleep some," he said quite clearly, and then seemed for a moment to fall asleep, as if he were ninety. But even as she watched, incredulous, he woke up again and said with lucidity, "Did you come here after me?"

"Who else? To cut Christmas trees, for Christsake? You stood me up for lunch yesterday."

"Oh." He stared, evidently trying to see her. "I'm sorry," he said, "I haven't been in my right mind."

Saying that, he was suddenly himself again, despite his lunatic hair and eyes: a man whose personal dignity went so deep as to be nearly invisible.

"It's all right. I don't care! But you're skipping therapy—aren't you?"

He nodded. "Would you like some coffee?" he asked. It was more than dignity. Integrity? Wholeness? Like a block of wood not carved.

The infinite possibility, the unlimited and unqualified wholeness of being of the uncommitted, the nonacting, the uncarved: the being who, being nothing but himself, is everything.

Briefly she saw him thus, and what struck her most, of that insight, was his strength. He was the strongest person she had ever known, because he could not be moved away from the center. And that was why she liked him. She was drawn to strength, came to it as a moth to light. She had had a good deal of love as a kid but no strength around her, nobody to lean on ever: people had leaned on her. Thirty years she had longed to meet somebody who didn't lean on her, who wouldn't ever, who couldn't. . . .

Here, short, bloodshot, psychotic, and in hiding, here he was, her tower of strength.

Life is the most incredible mess, Heather thought. You

95

never can guess what's next. She took off her coat, while Orr got a cup from the cabinet shelf and canned milk from the cupboard. He brought her a cup of powerful coffee: 97 per cent caffeine, 3 per cent free.

"None for you?"

"I've drunk too much. Gives me heartburn."

Her own heart went out to him entirely.

"What about brandy?"

He looked wistful.

"It won't put you to sleep. Jazz you up a bit. I'll go get it."

He flashlighted her back to the car. The creek shouted, the trees hung silent, the moon glowered overhead, the Aliens' moon.

Back in the cabin Orr poured out a modest shot of the brandy and tasted it. He shuddered. "That's good," he said, and drank it off.

She watched him with approval. "I always carry a pint flask," she said. "I stuck it in the glove compartment because if the fuzz stops me and I have to show my license it looks kind of funny in my handbag. But I mostly have it right on me. Funny how it comes in handy a couple of times every year."

"That's why you carry such a big handbag," Orr said, brandy-voiced.

"Damn right! I guess I'll put some in my coffee. It might weaken it." She refilled his glass at the same time. "How have you managed to stay awake for sixty or seventy hours?"

"I haven't entirely. I just didn't lie down. You can get some sleep sitting up but you can't really dream. You have to be lying down to get into dreaming sleep, so your big muscles can relax. Read that in books. It works pretty well. I haven't had a real dream yet. But not being able to relax wakes you up again. And then lately I get some sort of like hallucinations. Things wiggling on the wall."

"You can't keep that up!"

"No. I know. I just had to get away. From Haber." A pause. He seemed to have gone into another streak of grogginess. He gave a rather foolish laugh. "The only

96

solution I really can see," he said, "is to kill myself. But I don't want to. It just doesn't seem right."

"Of course it isn't right!"

"But I have to stop it somehow. I have to be stopped."

She could not follow him, and did not want to. "This is a nice place," she said. "I haven't smelled woodsmoke for twenty years."

"Plutes the air," he said, smiling feebly. He seemed to be quite gone; but she noticed he was holding himself in an erect sitting posture on the cot, not even leaning back against the wall. He blinked several times. "When you knocked," he said, "I thought it was a dream. That's why I mumble mumble coming."

"You said you dreamed yourself this cabin. Pretty modest for a dream. Why didn't you get yourself a beach chalet at Salishan, or a castle on Cape Perpetua?"

He shook his head frowning. "All I wanted." After blinking some more he said, "What happened. What happened to you. Friday. In Haber's office. The session."

"That's what I came to ask you!"

That woke him up. "You *were* aware—"

"I guess so. I mean, I know something happened. I sure have been trying to run on two tracks with one set of wheels ever since. I walked right into a wall Sunday in my own apartment! See?" She exhibited a bruise, blackish under brown skin, on her forehead. "The wall was *there* now but it wasn't there *now*. . . . How do you live with this going on all the time? How do you know where anything is?"

"I don't," Orr said. "I get all mixed up. If it's meant to happen at all it isn't meant to happen so often. It's too much. I can't tell any more whether I'm insane or just can't handle all the conflicting information. I . . . It . . . You mean you really believe me?"

"What else can I do? I saw what happened to the city! I was looking out the window! You needn't think I want to believe it. I don't, I try not to. Christ, it's terrible. But that Dr. Haber, he didn't want me to believe it either, did he? He sure did some fast talking. But then, what you said when you woke up; and then running into walls, and going to the wrong office. . . . Then I keep wondering, has he dreamed anything else since Friday, things are all changed again, but I don't know it because I wasn't there, and I keep wondering what things are changed, and whether anything's real at all. Oh shit, it's awful."

"That's it. Listen, you know the war—the war in the Near East?"

"Sure I know it. My husband was killed in it."

"Your husband?" He looked stricken. "When?"

"Just three days before they called it off. Two days before the Teheran Conference and the U.S.-China Pact. One day after the Aliens blew up the Moon base."

He was looking at her as if appalled.

"What's wrong? Oh, hell, it's an old scar. Six years ago, nearly seven. And if he'd lived we'd have been divorced by now, it was a lousy marriage. Look, it wasn't your fault!"

"I don't know what is my fault any more."

"Well, Jim sure wasn't. He was just a big handsome black unhappy son of a gun, bigshot Air Force Captain at 26 and shot down at 27, you don't think you invented that, do you, it's been happening for thousands of years. And it happened just exactly the same in that other— way, before Friday, when the world was so crowded. Just exactly. Only it was early in the war . . . wasn't it?" Her voice sank, softened. "My God. It was early in the war, instead of just before the cease-fire. That war went on and on. It was still going on right now. And there weren't . . . there weren't any Aliens—were there?"

Orr shook his head.

"Did you dream *them* up?"

"He made me dream about peace. Peace on earth, good will among men. So I made the Aliens. To give us something to fight."

"You didn't. That machine of his does it."

"No. I can do fine without the machine, Miss Lelache. All it does is save him time, getting me to dream right away. Although he's been working on it lately to improve it some way. He's great on improving things."

"Please call me Heather."

"It's a pretty name."

98

"Your name's George. He kept calling you George, in that session. Like you were a real clever poodle, or a rhesus monkey. Lie down, George. Dream this, George."

He laughed. His teeth were white, and his laugh pleasant, breaking through dishevelment and confusion. "That's not me. That's my subconscious, see, he's talking to. It is kind of like a dog or a monkey, for his purposes. It's not rational, but it can be trained to perform."

He never spoke with any bitterness at all, no matter how awful the things he said. Are there really people without resentment, without hate, she wondered. People who never go cross-grained to the universe? Who recognize evil, and resist evil, and yet are utterly unaffected by it?

Of course there are. Countless, the living and the dead. Those who have returned in pure compassion to the wheel, those who follow the way that cannot be followed without knowing they follow it, the sharecropper's wife in Alabama and the lama in Tibet and the entomologist in Peru and the millworker in Odessa and the greengrocer in London and the goatherd in Nigeria and the old, old man sharpening a stick by a dry streambed somewhere in Australia, and all the others. There is not one of us who has not known them. There are enough of them, enough to keep us going. Perhaps.

"Now look. Tell me, I need to know this: was it after you went to Haber that you started having. . . ."

"Effective dreams. No, before. It's why I went. I was scared of the dreams, so I was getting sedatives illegally to suppress dreaming. I didn't know what to do."

"Why didn't you take something these last two nights, then, instead of trying to keep awake?"

"I used up all I had Friday night. I can't fill the prescription here. But I had to get away. I wanted to get clear away from Dr. Haber. Things are more complicated than he's willing to realize. He thinks you can make things come out right. And he tries to use me to make things come out right, but he won't admit it; he lies because he won't look straight, he's not interested in what's true, in what is, he can't see anything except his mind—his ideas of what ought to be."

99

"Well. I can't do anything for you, as a lawyer," Heather said, not following this very well; she sipped her coffee and brandy, which would have grown hair on a Chihuahua. "There wasn't anything fishy in his hypnotic directions, that I could see; he just told you not to worry about overpopulation and stuff. And if he's determined to hide the fact that he's using your dreams for peculiar purposes, he can; using hypnosis he could just make sure you didn't have an effective dream while anybody else was watching. I wonder why he let me witness one? Are you sure he believes in them himself? I don't understand him. But anyway, it's hard for a lawyer to interfere between a psychiatrist and his patient, especially when the shrink is a big shot and the patient is a nut who thinks his dreams come true—no, I don't want this in court! But look. Isn't there any way you could keep yourself from dreaming for him? Tranquilizers, maybe?"

"I haven't got a Pharm Card while I'm on VTT. He'd have to prescribe them. Anyway, his Augmentor could get me dreaming."

"It *is* invasion of privacy; but it won't make a case. . . . Listen. What if you had a dream where you changed *him?*"

Orr stared at her through a fog of sleep and brandy.

"Made him more benevolent—well, you say he is benevolent, that he means well. But he's power-hungry. He's found a great way to run the world without taking any responsibility for it. Well. Make him less power-hungry. Dream that he's a *really* good man. Dream that he's trying to cure you, not use you!"

"But I can't choose my dreams. Nobody can."

She sagged. "I forgot. As soon as I accept this thing as real, I keep thinking it's something you can control. But you can't. You just *do* it."

"I don't do anything," Orr said morosely. "I never have done anything. I just dream. And then it is."

"I'll hypnotize you," Heather said suddenly.

To have accepted an incredible fact as true gave her a rather heady feeling: if Orr's dreams worked, what else mightn't work? Also she had eaten nothing since noon, and the coffee and brandy were hitting hard.

He stared some more.

"I've done it. Took psych courses in college, in pre-law. We all worked out both as hypnotizers and subjects, in one course. I was a fair subject, but real good at putting the others under. I'll put you under, and suggest a dream to you. About Dr. Haber—making him harmless. I'll tell you just to dream that, nothing more. See? Wouldn't that be safe—as safe as anything we could try, at this point?"

"But I'm hypnosis-resistant. I didn't use to be, but he says I am now."

"Is that why he uses vagus-carotid induction? I hate to watch that, it looks like a murder. I couldn't do that, I'm not a doctor, anyway."

"My dentist used to just use a Hypnotape. It worked fine. At least I think it did." He was absolutely talking in his sleep and might have maundered on indefinitely.

She said gently, "It sounds like you're resisting the hypnotist, not the hypnosis. . . . We could try it, anyhow. And if it worked, I could give you posthypnotic suggestion to dream one small what d'you call it, effective, dream about Haber. So he'll come clean with you, and try to help you. Do you think that might work? Would you trust it?"

"I could get some sleep, anyway," he said. "I . . . will have to sleep sometime. I don't think I can go through tonight. If you think you could do the hypnosis . . ."

"I think I can. But listen, have you got anything to eat here?"

"Yes," he said drowsily. After some while he came to. "Oh yes. I'm sorry. You didn't eat. Getting here. There's a loaf of bread. . . ." He rooted in the cupboard, brought out bread, margarine, five hard-boiled eggs, a can of tuna, and some shopworn lettuce. She found two tin pie plates, three various forks, and a paring knife. "Have you eaten?" she demanded. He was not sure. They made a meal together, she sitting in the chair at the table, he standing. Standing up seemed to revive him, and he proved a hungry eater. They had to divide everything in half, even the fifth egg.

"You are a very kind person," he said.

"Me? Why? Coming here, you mean? Oh shit, I was scared. By that world-changing bit on Friday! I had to get it straight. Look, I was looking right at the hospital I was *born* in, across the river, when you were dreaming, and then all of a sudden it wasn't there and never had been!"

"I thought you were from the East," he said. Relevance was not his strong point at the moment.

"No." She cleaned out the tuna can scrupulously and licked the knife. "Portland. Twice, now. Two different hospitals. Christ! But born and bred. So were my parents. My father was black and my mother was white. It's kind of interesting. He was a real militant Black Power type, back in the seventies, you know, and she was a hippie. He was from a welfare family in Albina, no father, and she was a corporation lawyer's daughter from Portland Heights. And a dropout, and went on drugs, and all that stuff they used to do then. And they met at some political rally, demonstrating. That was when demonstrations were still legal. And they got married. But he couldn't stick it very long, I mean the whole situation, not just the marriage. When I was eight he went off to Africa. To Ghana, I think. He thought his people came originally from there, but he didn't really know. They'd been in Louisiana since anybody knew, and Lelache would be the slaveowner's name, it's French. It means The Coward. I took French in high school because I had a French name." She snickered. "Anyway, he just went. And poor Eva sort of fell apart. That's my mother. She never wanted me to call her Mother or Mom or anything, that was middle-class nucleus family possessiveness. So I called her Eva. And we lived in a sort of commune thing for a while up on Mount Hood, oh Christ! Was it cold in winter! But the police broke it up, they said it was an anti-American conspiracy. And after that she sort of scrounged a living, she made nice pottery when she could get the use of somebody's wheel and kiln, but mostly she helped out in little stores and restaurants, and stuff. Those people helped each other a lot. A real lot. But she never could keep off the hard drugs, she was hooked. She'd be off for a year and then bingo. She got through the Plague, but when she was thirty-eight she got a dirty needle, and it killed her. And damn if her *family* didn't show up and take me over. I'd never even seen them! And they put me through college and law school. And I go up there for Christmas Eve dinner every year. I'm their token Negro. But I'll tell you, what really gets me is, I can't decide which color I am. I mean, my father was a black, a real black—oh, he had some white blood, but he was a *black*—and my mother was a white, and I'm neither one. See, my father really hated my mother because she was white. But he also loved her. But I think she loved his being black much more than she loved *him*. Well, where does that leave me? I never have figured out."

"Brown," he said gently, standing behind her chair.

"Shit color."

"The color of the earth."

"Are you a Portlander? Equal time."

"Yes."

"I can't hear you over that damn creek. I thought the wilderness was supposed to be silent. Go on!"

"But I've had so many childhoods, now," he said. "Which one should I tell you about? In one both my parents died in the first year of the Plague. In one there wasn't any Plague. I don't know. . . . None of them were very interesting. I mean, nothing to tell. All I ever did was survive."

"Well. That's the main thing."

"It gets harder all the time. The Plague, and now the Aliens . . ." He gave a feckless laugh, but when she looked around at him his face was weary and miserable.

"I can't believe you dreamed them up. I just can't. I've been scared of them for so long, six years! But I knew you did, as soon as I thought about it, because they weren't in that other—time-track or whatever it is. But actually, they aren't any worse than that awful overcrowding. That horrible little flat I lived in, with four other women, in a Business Girls Condominium, for Christsake! And riding that ghastly subway, and my teeth were terrible, and there never was anything decent to eat, and not half enough either. Do you know, I weighed 101 then, and I'm 122 now. I gained twenty-one pounds since Friday!"

"That's right. You were awfully thin, that first time I saw you. In your law office."

"You were, too. You looked scrawny. Only everybody else did, so I didn't notice it. Now you look like you'd be a fairly solid type, if you ever got any sleep."

He said nothing.

"Everybody else looks a lot better, too, when you come to think of it. Look. If you can't help what you do, and what you do makes things a little better, then you shouldn't feel any guilt about it. Maybe your dreams are just a new way for evolution to act, sort of. A hot line. Survival of the fittest and all. With crash priority."

"Oh, worse than that," he said in the same airy, foolish tone; he sat down on the bed. "Do you—" He stuttered several times. "Do you remember anything about April, four years ago—in '98?"

"April? No, nothing special."

"That's when the world ended," Orr said. A muscular spasm disfigured his face, and he gulped as if for air. "Nobody else remembers," he said.

"What do you mean?" she asked, obscurely frightened. April, April 1998, she thought, do I remember April '98? She thought she did not, and knew she must; and she was frightened—by him? With him? For him?

"It isn't evolution. It's just self-preservation. I can't— Well, it was a lot worse. Worse than you remember. It was the same world as that first one you remember, with a population of seven billion, only it—it was worse. Nobody but some of the European countries got rationing and pollution control and birth control going early enough, in the seventies, and so when we finally did try to control food distribution it was too late, there wasn't enough, and the Mafia ran the black market, everybody had to buy on the black market to get anything to eat, and a lot of people didn't get anything. They rewrote the Constitution in 1984, the way you remember, but things were so bad by then that it was a lot worse, it didn't even pretend to be a democracy any more, it was a sort of police state, but it didn't work, it fell apart right away. When I was fifteen the schools closed. There wasn't any Plague, but there were epidemics, one after another, dysentery and hepatitis and then bubonic. But mostly

104

people starved. And then in '93 the war started up in the Near East, but it was different. It was Israel against the Arabs and Egypt. All the big countries got in on it. One of the African states came in on the Arab side, and used nuclear bombs on two cities in Israel, and so we helped them retaliate, and. . . ." He was silent for some while and then went on, apparently not realizing that there was any gap in his telling, "I was trying to get out of the city. I wanted to get into Forest Park. I was sick, I couldn't go on walking and I sat down on the steps of this house up in the west hills, the houses were all burnt out but the steps were cement, I remember there were some dandelions flowering in a crack between the steps. I sat there and I couldn't get up again and I knew I couldn't. I kept thinking that I was standing up and going on, getting out of the city, but it was just delirium, I'd come to and see the dandelions again and know I was dying. And that everything else was dying. And then I had the—I had this dream." His voice had hoarsened; now it choked off.

"I was all right," he said at last. "I dreamed about being home. I woke up and I was all right. I was in bed at home. Only it wasn't any home I'd ever had, the other time, the first time. The bad time. Oh God, I wish I didn't remember it. I mostly don't. I can't. I've told myself ever since that it was a dream. That *it* was a dream! But it wasn't. This is. This isn't real. This world isn't even probable. It was the truth. It was what happened. We are all dead, and we spoiled the world before we died. There is nothing left. Nothing but dreams."

She believed him, and denied her belief with fury. "So what? Maybe that's all it's ever been! Whatever it is, it's all right. You don't suppose you'd be allowed to do anything you weren't supposed to do, do you? Who the hell do you think you are! There is nothing that doesn't fit, nothing happens that isn't supposed to happen. Ever! What does it matter whether you call it real or dreams? It's all one— isn't it?"

"I don't know," Orr said in agony; and she went to him and held him as she would have held a child in pain, or a dying man.

The head on her shoulder was heavy, the fair, square hand on her knee lay relaxed.

"You're asleep," she said. He made no denial. She had to shake him pretty hard to get him even to deny it. "No I'm not," he said, starting and sitting upright. "No." He sagged again.

"George!" It was true: the use of his name helped. He kept his eyes open long enough to look at her. "Stay awake, stay awake just a little. I want to try the hypnosis. So you can sleep." She had meant to ask him what he wanted to dream, what she should impress on him hypnotically concerning Haber, but he was too far gone now. "Look, sit there on the cot. Look at . . . look at the flame of the lamp, that ought to do it. But don't go to sleep." She set the oil lamp on the center of the table, amidst eggshells and wreckage. "Just keep your eyes on it, and don't go to sleep! You'll relax and feel easy, but you won't go to sleep yet, not till I say 'Go to sleep.' That's it. Now you're feeling easy and comfortable. . . ." With a sense of play acting, she proceeded with the hypnotist's spiel. He went under almost at once. She couldn't believe it, and tested him. "You can't lift your left hand," she said, "you're trying, but it's too heavy, it won't come. . . . Now it's light again, you can lift it. There . . . well. In a minute now you're going to fall asleep. You'll dream some, but they'll just be regular ordinary dreams like everybody has, not special ones, not—not effective ones. All except one. You'll have one effective dream. In it—" She halted. All of a sudden she was scared; a cold qualm took her. What was she doing? This was no play, no game, nothing for a fool to meddle in. He was in her power: and his power was incalculable. What unimaginable responsibility had she undertaken?

A person who believes, as she did, that things fit: that there is a whole of which one is a part, and that in being a part one is whole: such a person has no desire whatever, at any time, to play God. Only those who have denied their being yearn to play at it.

But she was caught in a role and couldn't back out of it now. "In that one dream, you'll dream that . . . that Dr.

Haber is benevolent, that he's not trying to hurt you and will be honest with you." She didn't know what to say, how to say it, knowing that whatever she said could go wrong. "And you'll dream that the Aliens aren't out there on the Moon any longer," she added hastily; she could get that load off his shoulders, anyhow. "And in the morning you'll wake up quite rested, everything will be all right. Now: Go to sleep."

Oh shit, she'd forgotten to tell him to lie down first.

He went like a half-stuffed pillow, softly, forward and sideways, till he was a large, warm, inert heap on the floor.

He couldn't have weighed more than 150, but he might have been a dead elephant for all the help he gave her getting him up on the cot. She had to do it legs first and then heave the shoulders, so as not to tip the cot; he ended up on the sleeping bag, of course, not in it. She dragged it out from under him, nearly tipping over the cot again, and got it spread out over him. He slept, slept utterly, through it all. She was out of breath, sweating, and upset. He wasn't.

She sat down at the table and got her breath. After a while she wondered what to do. She cleaned up their dinner-leavings, heated water, washed the pie tins, forks, knife, and cups. She built up the fire in the stove. She found several books on a shelf, paperbacks he'd picked up in Lincoln City probably, to beguile his long vigil. No mysteries, hell, a good mystery was what she needed. There was a novel about Russia. One thing about the Space Pact: the U.S. Government wasn't trying to pretend that nothing between Jerusalem and the Philippines existed because if it did it might threaten the American Way of Life; and so these last few years you could buy Japanese toy paper parasols, and Indian incense, and Russian novels, and things, once more. Human Brotherhood was the New Life-Style, according to President Merdle.

This book, by somebody with a name ending in "evsky", was about life during the Plague Years in a little town in the Caucasus, and it wasn't exactly jolly reading, but it caught at her emotions; she read it from ten o'clock till two-thirty. All that time Orr lay fast asleep, scarcely moving, breathing lightly and quietly. She would look up from the Caucasian village and see his face, gilt and shadowed in the dim lamplight, serene. If he dreamed, they were quiet dreams and fleeting. After everybody in the Caucasian village was dead except the village idiot (whose perfect passivity to the inevitable kept making her think of her companion), she tried some rewarmed coffee, but it tasted like lye. She went to the door and stood half inside, half outside for a while, listening to the creek shouting and hollering eternal praise! eternal praise! It was incredible that it had kept up that tremendous noise for hundreds of years before she was even born, and would go on doing it until the mountains moved. And the strangest thing about it, now very late at night in the absolute silence of the woods, was a distant note in it, far away upstream it seemed, like the voices of children singing— very sweet, very strange.

She got shivery; she shut the door on the voices of the unborn children singing in the water, and turned to the small warm room and the sleeping man. She took down a book on home carpentry which he had evidently bought to keep himself busy about the cabin, but it put her to sleep at once. Well, why not? Why did she have to stay up? But where was she supposed to sleep. . . .

She should have left George on the floor. He never would have noticed. It wasn't fair, he had both the cot and the sleeping bag.

She removed the sleeping bag from him, replacing it with his raincoat and her raincape. He never stirred. She looked at him with affection, then got into the sleeping bag down on the floor. Christ it was cold down here on the floor, and hard. She hadn't blown out the light. Or did you turn out wick lamps? You should do one and shouldn't do the other. She remembered that from the commune. But she couldn't remember which. Oooooh SHIT it was cold down here!

Cold, cold. Hard. Bright. Too bright. Sunrise in the window through shift and flicker of trees. Over the bed. The floor trembled. The hills muttered and dreamed of
108

falling in the sea, and over the hills, faint and horrible, the sirens of distant towns howled, howled, howled.

She sat up. The wolves howled for the world's end.

Sunrise poured in through the single window, hiding all that lay under its dazzling slant. She felt through excess of light and found the dreamer sprawled on his face, still sleeping. "George! Wake up! Oh, George, please wake up! Something is wrong!"

He woke. He smiled at her, waking.

"Something is *wrong*—the sirens—what is it?"

Still almost in his dream, he said without emotion, "They've landed."

For he had done just what she told him to do. She had told him to dream that the Aliens were no longer on the Moon.

8

Heaven and Earth are not humane.
—Lao Tse: V

In the Second World War the only part of the American mainland to suffer direct attack was the State of Oregon. Some Japanese fire balloons set a piece of forest burning on the coast. In the First Interstellar War the only part of the American mainland to be invaded was the State of Oregon. One might lay the blame on her politicians; the historic function of a Senator from Oregon is to drive all the other Senators mad, and no military butter is ever put upon the state bread. Oregon had no stockpiles of anything but hay, no missile launch pads, no NASA bases. She was obviously defenseless. The Anti-Alien Ballistic Missiles defending her went up from the enormous underground installations in Walla Walla, Washington, and Round Valley, California. From Idaho, most of which belonged to the U.S. Air Force, huge supersonic XXTT-9900s went screaming west, shattering every eardrum from Boise to Sun Valley, to patrol for any Alien ship that might somehow slip through the infallible network of the AABMs.

Repelled by the Alien ships, which carried a device that took control of the missiles' guidance systems, the AABMs turned around somewhere in the middle stratosphere and returned, landing and exploding here and there over the State of Oregon. Holocausts raged on the dry eastern slopes of the Cascades. Gold Beach and the Dalles were wiped out by fire storms. Portland was not directly hit; but an errant nuclear-warhead AABM striking Mount Hood near the old crater caused the dormant volcano to

110

wake up. Steam and ground tremors ensued at once, and by noon of the first day of the Alien Invasion, April Fools' Day, a vent had opened on the northwestern side and was in violent eruption. Lava flow set the snowless, deforested slopes blazing, and threatened the communities of Zigzag and Rhododendron. A cinder cone began to form, and the air in Portland, forty miles away, was soon thickening and gray with ash. As evening came and the wind changed round to the south, the lower air cleared somewhat, revealing the somber orange flicker of the eruption in the eastern clouds. The sky, full of rain and ashes, thundered with the flights of XXTT-9900s vainly seeking Alien ships. Other flights of bombers and fighters were still coming in from the East Coast and from fellow nations of the Pact; these frequently shot each other down. The ground shook with earthquake and the impact of bombs and plane crashes. One of the Alien ships had landed only eight miles from the city limits, and so the southwestern outskirts of town were pulverized, as jet bombers methodically devastated the eleven-square-mile area in which the Alien ship was said to have been. As a matter of fact information had arrived that it was no longer there. But something had to be done. Bombs fell by mistake on many other parts of the city, as will happen with jet bombing. There was no glass left in any window downtown. It lay, instead, in all the downtown streets, in small fragments, an inch or two deep. Refugees from southwest Portland had to walk through it; women carried their children and walked weeping with pain, in thin shoes full of broken glass.

William Haber stood at the great window of his office in the Oregon Oneirological Institute watching the fires flare and wane down in the docks, and the bloody lightning of the eruption. There was still glass in that window; nothing had landed or exploded yet near Washington Park, and the ground tremors that cracked open whole buildings down in the river bottoms so far had done nothing worse up in the hills than rattle the window frames. Very faintly he could hear elephants screaming, over in the zoo. Streaks of an unusual purplish light showed occasionally to the north, perhaps over the area where the Willamette joins the Columbia; it was hard to locate anything for certain in the ashy, misty twilight. Large sections of the city were blacked out by power failure; other parts twinkled faintly, though the streetlights had not been turned on.

No one else was in the Institute Building.

Haber had spent all day trying to locate George Orr. When his search proved futile, and further search was made impossible by the hysteria and increasing dilapidation of the city, he had come up to the Institute. He had had to walk most of the way, and had found the experience unnerving. A man in his position, with so many calls on his time, of course drove a batcar. But the battery gave out and he couldn't get to a recharger because the crowds in the street were so thick. He had to get out and walk, against the current of the crowd, facing them all, right in amongst them. That had been distressing. He did not like crowds. But then the crowds had ceased and he was left walking all alone in the vast expanses of lawn and grove and forest of the Park: and that was a great deal worse.

Haber considered himself a lone wolf. He had never wanted marriage nor close friendships, he had chosen a strenuous research carried out when others sleep, he had avoided entanglements. He kept his sex life almost entirely to one-night stands, semipros, sometimes women and sometimes young men; he knew which bars and cinemas and saunas to go to for what he wanted. He got what he wanted and got clear again, before he or the other person could possibly develop any kind of need for the other. He prized his independence, his free will.

But he found it terrible to be alone, all alone in the huge indifferent Park, hurrying, almost running, toward the Institute, because he did not have anywhere else to go. He got there and it was all silent, all deserted.

Miss Crouch kept a transistor radio in her desk drawer. He got this, and kept it on softly so he could hear the latest reports, or anyway hear a human voice.

Everything he needed was here; beds, dozens of them, food, the sandwich and soft-drink machines for the all-night workers in the sleep labs. But he was not hungry. He

112

felt instead a kind of apathy. He listened to the radio, but it would not listen to him. He was all alone, and nothing seemed to be real in solitude. He needed somebody, anybody, to talk to, he had to tell them what he felt so that he knew if he felt anything. This horror of being by himself was strong enough that it almost drove him out of the Institute and down into the crowds again, but the apathy was still stronger than the fear. He did nothing, and the night darkened.

Over Mount Hood the reddish glow sometimes spread enormously, then paled again. Something big hit, in the southwest of town, out of view from his office; and soon the clouds were lit from beneath with a livid glare that seemed to rise from that direction. Haber was going out into the corridor to see what could be seen, carrying the radio with him. People were coming up the stairs, he had not heard them. For a moment he merely stared at them.

"Dr. Haber," one of them said.

It was Orr. "It's about time," Haber said bitterly. "Where the hell have you been all day? Come on!"

Orr came up limping; the left side of his face was swollen and bloody, his lip was cut, and he had lost half a front tooth. The woman with him looked less battered but more exhausted: glassy-eyed, knees giving. Orr made her sit down on the couch in the office. Haber said in a loud medical voice, "She get a blow on the head?"

"No. It's been a long day."

"I'm all right," the woman mumbled, shivering a little. Orr was quick and solicitous, taking off her repulsively muddy shoes and putting the camel's-hair blanket from the foot of the couch over her; Haber wondered who she was, but gave it only the one thought. He was beginning to function again. "Let her rest there, she'll be all right. Come here, clean yourself up. I spent the whole day looking for you. Where were you?"

"Trying to get back to town. There was some kind of bombing pattern we ran into, they blew up the road just ahead of the car. Car bounced around a lot. Turned over, I guess. Heather was behind me, and stopped in time, so her car was all right and we came on in it. But we had to cut

113

over to the Sunset Highway because 99 was all blown up, and then we had to leave the car at a roadblock out near the bird sanctuary. So we walked in through the Park."

"Where the hell were you coming from?" Haber had run hot water in his private washroom sink, and now gave Orr a steaming towel to hold to his bloody face.

"Cabin. In the Coast Range."

"What's wrong with your leg?"

"Bruised it when the car turned over, I guess. Listen, are they in the city yet?"

"If the military knows, it's not telling. All they'll say is that when the big ships landed this mornnig they split into small mobile units, something like helicopters, and scattered. They're all over the western half of the state. They're reported to be slow-moving, but if they're shooting them down, they don't report it."

"We saw one," Orr's face emerged from the towel, marked with purple bruises, but less shocking now the blood and mud were off. "That's what it must have been. Little silvery thing, about thirty feet up, over a pasture near North Plains. It seemed to sort of hop along. Didn't look earthly. Are the Aliens fighting us, are they shooting planes down?"

"The radio doesn't say. No losses are reported, except civilians. Now come on, let's get some coffee and food into you. And then, by God, we'll have a therapy session in the middle of Hell, and put an end to this idiotic mess you've made." He had prepared a shot of sodium pentothal, and now took Orr's arm and gave him the shot without warning or apology.

"That's why I came here. But I don't know if—"

"If you can do it? You can. Come on!" Orr was hovering over the woman again. "She's all right. She's asleep, don't bother her, it's what she needs. Come on!" He took Orr down to the food machines, and got him a roast beef sandwich, an egg and tomato sandwich, two apples, four chocolate bars, and two cups of coffee with. They sat down at a table in Sleep Lab One, sweeping aside a Patience layout that had been abandoned at dawn when the sirens began to howl. "O.K. Eat. Now, in case you
114

think that clearing up this mess is beyond you, forget it. I've been working on the Augmentor, and it can do it for you. I've got the model, the template, of your brain emissions during effective dreaming. Where I went wrong all month was in looking for an entity, an Omega Wave. There isn't one. It's simply a pattern formed by the combination of other waves, and over this last couple of days, before all hell broke loose, I finally worked it out. The cycle is ninety-seven seconds. That means nothing to you, even though it's your goddamn brain doing it. Put it this way, when you're dreaming effectively your entire brain is involved in a complexly synchronized pattern of emissions that takes ninety-seven seconds to complete itself and start again, a kind of counterpoint effect that is to ordinary d-state graphs what Beethoven's Great Fugue is to Mary Had a Little Lamb. It is incredibly complex, yet it's consistent and it recurs. Therefore I can feed it to you straight, and amplified. The Augmentor's all set up, it's ready for you, it's really going to fit the inside of your head at last! When you dream this time, you'll dream big, baby. Big enough to stop this crazy invasion, and get us clean over into another continuum, where we can start fresh. That's what you do, you know. You don't change things, or lives, you shift the whole continuum."

"It's nice to be able to talk about it with you," Orr said, or something like it; he had eaten the sandwiches incredibly fast, despite his cut mouth and broken tooth, and was now engulfing a chocolate bar. There was irony, or something, in what he said, but Haber was much too busy to bother about it.

"Listen. Did this invasion just happen, or did it happen because you missed an appointment?"

"I dreamed it."

"You let yourself have an uncontrolled effective dream?" Haber let the heavy anger lie in his voice. He had been too protective, too easy on Orr. Orr's irresponsibility was the cause of the death of many innocent people, the wreckage and panic loose in the city: he must face up to what he had done.

"It wasn't," Orr was just beginning, when a really big

115

explosion hit. The building jumped, rang, crackled, electronic apparatus leaped about by the row of empty beds, coffee slopped in the cups. "Was that the volcano or the Air Force?" Orr said, and in the midst of the natural dismay the explosion had caused him, Haber noticed that Orr seemed quite undismayed. His reactions were utterly abnormal. On Friday he had been going all to pieces over a mere ethical point; here on Wednesday in the midst of Armageddon he was cool and calm. He seemed to have no personal fear. But he must have. If Haber was afraid, of course Orr must be. He was suppressing fear. Or did he think, Haber suddenly wondered, that because he had dreamed the invasion, it was all just a dream?

What if it *was?*

Whose?

"We'd better get back upstairs," Haber said, getting up. He felt increasingly impatient and irritable; the excitement was getting too extensive. "Who's the woman with you, anyway?"

"That's Miss Lelache," Orr said, looking at him oddly. "The lawyer. She was here Friday."

"How'd she happen to be with you?"

"She was looking for me, came to the cabin after me."

"You can explain all that later," Haber said. There was no time to waste on this trivia. They had to get out, to get out of this burning exploding world.

Just as they entered Haber's office the glass burst out of the great double window with a shrill, singing sound and a huge sucking-out of air; both men were impelled toward the window as if toward the mouth of a vacuum cleaner. Everything then turned white: everything. They both fell over.

Neither was aware of any noise.

When he could see again, Haber scrambled up, holding on to his desk. Orr was already over by the couch, trying to reassure the bewildered woman. It was cold in the office: the spring air had a moist chill in it, pouring in the empty windows, and it smelled of smoke, burnt insulation, ozone, sulfur, and death. "We ought to get down into the

116

basement, don't you think?" Miss Lelache said in a reasonable tone, though she was shivering hard.

"Go on," Haber said. "We've got to stay up here a while."

"Stay here?"

"The Augmentor's here. It doesn't plug in and out like a portable TV! Get on down into the basement, we'll join you when we can."

"You're going to put him to sleep *now?*" the woman said, as the trees down the hill suddenly burst into bright yellow balls of flame. The eruption of Mount Hood was quite hidden by events closer at hand; the earth, however, had been trembling gently for the past few minutes, a sort of fundamental palsy that made one's hands and mind shake sympathetically.

"You're fucking right I am. Go on. Get down to the basement, I need the couch. Lie down, George. . . . Listen, you, in the basement just past the janitor's room you'll see a door marked Emergency Generator. Go in there, find the ON handle. Have your hand on it, and if the lights fail, turn it on. It'll take a heavy pressure upward on the handle. Go on!"

She went. She was still shaking, and smiling; as she went she caught Orr's hand for a second and said, "Pleasant dreams, George."

"Don't worry," Orr said, "It's all right."

"Shut up," Haber snapped. He had switched on the Hypnotape he had recorded himself, but Orr wasn't even paying attention, and the noise of explosions and things burning made it hard to hear. "Shut your eyes!" Haber commanded, put his hand on Orr's throat, and turned up the gain. "RELAXING," said his own huge voice. "YOU FEEL COMFORTABLE AND RELAXED. YOU WILL ENTER THE—" The building leaped like a spring lamb and settled down askew. Something appeared in the dirty-red, opaque glare outside the glassless window: an ovoid, large object, moving in a sort of hopping fashion through the air. It came directly toward the window. "We've got to get out!" Haber shouted over his own voice, and then realized that Orr was already hypnotized. He snapped the tape off and leaned down so he could speak in Orr's ear. "Stop the invasion!" he shouted. "Peace, peace, dream that we're at peace with *everybody!* Now sleep! Antwerp!" and he switched on the Augmentor.

But he had no time to look at Orr's EEG. The ovoid shape was hovering directly outside the window. Its blunt snout, lit luridly by reflections of the burning city, pointed straight at Haber. He cowered down by the couch, feeling horribly soft and exposed, trying to protect the Augmentor with his inadequate flesh, stretching out his arms across it. He craned over his shoulder to watch the Alien ship. It pressed closer. The snout, looking like oily steel, silver with violet streaks and gleams, filled the entire window. There was a crunching, racking sound as it jammed itself into the frame. Haber sobbed aloud with terror, but stayed spread out there between the Alien and the Augmentor.

The snout, halting, emitted a long thin tentacle which moved about questingly in the air. The end of it, rearing like a cobra, pointed at random, then settled in Haber's direction. About ten feet from him, it hung in the air and pointed at him for some seconds. Then it withdrew with a hiss and crack like a carpenter's flexible rule, and a high, humming noise came from the ship. The metal sill of the window screeched and buckled. The ship's snout whirled around and fell off onto the floor. From the hole that gaped behind it, something emerged.

It was, Haber thought in emotionless horror, a giant turtle. Then he realized that it was encased in a suit of some kind, which gave it a bulky, greenish, armored, inexpressive look like a giant sea turtle standing on its hind legs.

It stood quite still, near Haber's desk. Very slowly it raised its left arm, pointing at him a metallic, nozzled instrument.

He faced death.

A flat, toneless voice came out of the elbow joint. "Do not do to others what you wish others not to do to you," it said.

Haber stared, his heart faltering.

118

The huge, heavy, metallic arm came up again. "We are attempting to make peaceful arrival," the elbow said all on one note. "Please inform others that this is peaceful arrival. We do not have any weapons. Great self-destruction follows upon unfounded fear. Please cease destruction of self and others. We do not have any weapons. We are nonaggressive unfighting species."

"I—I—I can't control the Air Force," Haber stammered.

"Persons in flying vehicles are being contacted presently," the creature's elbow joint said. "Is this a military installation?"

Word order showed it to be a question. "No," Haber said, "No, nothing of the kind—"

"Please then excuse unwarranted intrusion." The huge, armored figure whirred slightly and seemed to hesitate. "What is device?" it said, pointing with its right elbow joint at the machinery connected to the head of the sleeping man.

"An electroencephalograph, a machine which records the electrical activity of the brain—"

"Worthy," said the Alien, and took a short, checked step toward the couch, as if longing to look. "The individual-person is *iahklu'*. The recording machine records this perhaps. Is all your species capable of *iahklu'*?"

"I don't—don't know the term, can you describe—"

The figure whirred a little, raised its left elbow over its head (which, turtle-like, hardly protruded above the great sloped shoulders of the carapace), and said, "Please excuse. Incommunicable by communication-machine invented hastily in very-recent-past. Please excuse. It is necessary that all we proceed in very-near-future rapidly toward other responsible individual-persons engaged in panic and capable of destroying selves and others. Thank you very much." And it crawled back into the nose of the ship.

Haber watched the great, round soles of its feet disappear into the dark cavity.

The nose cone jumped up from the floor and twirled itself smartly into place: Haber had a vivid impression that it was not acting mechanically, but temporally, repeating its previous actions in reverse, precisely like a film run backward. The Alien ship, jarring the office and tearing out the rest of the window frame with a hideous noise, withdrew, and vanished into the lurid murk outside.

The crescendo of explosions, Haber now realized, had ceased; in fact it was fairly quiet. Everything trembled a little, but that would be the mountain, not the bombs. Sirens whooped, far and desolate, across the river.

George Orr lay inert on the couch, breathing irregularly, the cuts and swellings on his face looking ugly on his pallor. Cinders and fumes still drifted in the chill, choking air through the smashed window. Nothing had been changed. He had undone nothing. Had he done anything yet? There was a slight eye movement under the closed lids; he was still dreaming; he could not do otherwise, with the Augmentor overriding the impulses of his own brain. Why didn't he change continuums, why didn't he get them into a peaceful world, as Haber had told him to do? The hypnotic suggestion hadn't been clear or strong enough. They must start all over. Haber switched off the Augmentor, and spoke Orr's name thrice.

"Don't sit up, the Augmentor hookup's still on you. What did you dream?"

Orr spoke huskily and slowly, not fully awakened. "The . . . an Alien was here. In here. In the office. It came out of the nose of one of their hopping ships. In the window. You and it were talking together."

"But that's not a dream! That happened! Goddamn, we'll have to do this over again. That might have been an atomic blast a few minutes ago, we've got to get into another continuum, we may all be dead of radiation exposure already—"

"Oh, not this time," Orr said, sitting up and combing off electrodes as if they were dead lice. "Of course it happened. An effective dream is a reality, Dr. Haber."

Haber stared at him.

"I suppose your Augmentor increased the immediacy of it for you," Orr said, still with extraordinary calmness. He appeared to ponder for a little. "Listen, couldn't you call Washington?"

"What for?"

"Well, a famous scientist right here in the middle of it all might get listened to. They'll be looking for explanations. Is there somebody in the government you know, that you might call? Maybe the HEW Minister? You could tell him that the whole thing's a misunderstanding, the Aliens aren't invading or attacking. They simply didn't realize until they landed that humans depend on *verbal* communication. They didn't even know we thought we were at war with them. . . . If you could tell somebody who can get the President's ear. The sooner Washington can call off the military, the fewer people will be killed here. It's only civilians getting killed. The Aliens aren't hurting the soldiers, they aren't even armed, and I have the impression that they're indestructible, in those suits. But if somebody doesn't stop the Air Force, they'll blow up the whole city. Give it a try, Dr. Haber. They might listen to you."

Haber felt that Orr was right. There was no reason to it, it was the logic of insanity, but there it was: his chance. Orr spoke with the incontrovertible conviction of dream, in which there is no free will: do this, you must do it, it is to be done.

Why had this gift been given to a fool, a passive nothing of a man? Why was Orr so sure and so right, while the strong, active, positive man was powerless, forced to try to use, even to obey, the weak tool? This went through his mind, not for the first time, but even as he thought it he was going over to the desk, to the telephone. He sat down and dialed direct-distance to the HEW offices in Washington. The call, handled through the Federal Telephone switchboards in Utah, went straight through.

While he was waiting to be put through to the Minister of Health, Education, and Welfare, whom he knew fairly well, he said to Orr, "Why didn't you put us over in another continuum where this mess simply never happened? It would be a lot easier. And nobody would be dead. Why didn't you simply get *rid* of the Aliens?"

"I don't choose," Orr said. "Don't you see that yet? I follow."

"You follow my hypnotic suggestions, yes, but never fully, never directly and simply—"

"I didn't mean those," Orr said, but Rantow's personal secretary was now on the line. While Haber was talking Orr slipped away, downstairs, no doubt, to see about the woman. That was all right. As he talked to the secretary and then to the Minister himself, Haber began to feel convinced that things were going to be all right now, that the Aliens were in fact totally unaggressive, and that he would be able to make Rantow believe this, and, through Rantow, the President and his Generals. Orr was no longer necessary. Haber saw what must be done, and would lead his country out of the mess.

9

Those who dream of feasting wake to lamendation.
—Chuang Tse: II

It was the third week in April. Orr had made a date, last week, to meet Heather Lelache at Dave's for lunch on Thursday, but as soon as he started out from his office he knew it wouldn't work.

There were by now so many different memories, so many skeins of life experience, jostling in his head, that he scarcely tried to remember anything. He took it as it came. He was living almost like a young child, among actualities only. He was surprised by nothing, and by everything.

His office was on the third floor of the Civil Planning Bureau; his position was more impressive than any he had had before: he was in charge of the South-East Suburban Parks section of the City Planning Commission. He did not like the job and never had.

He had always managed to remain some kind of draftsman, up until the dream last Monday that had, in juggling the Federal and State Governments around to suit some plan of Haber's, so thoroughly rearranged the whole social system that he had ended up as a City bureaucrat. He had never held a job, in any of his lives, which was quite up his alley; what he knew he was best at was design, the realization of proper and fitting shape and form for things, and this talent had not been in demand in any of his various existences. But this job, which he had (now) held and disliked for five years, was way out of line. That worried him.

Until this week there had been an essential continuity, a

coherence, among all the existences resultant from his dreams. He had always been some kind of draftsman, had always lived on Corbett Avenue. Even in the life that had ended on the concrete steps of a burnt-out house in a dying city in a ruined world, even in that life, up until there were no more jobs and no more homes, those continuities had held. And throughout all the subsequent dreams or lives, many more important things had also remained constant. He had improved the local climate a little, but not much, and the Greenhouse Effect remained, a permanent legacy of the middle of the last century. Geography remained perfectly steady: the continents were where they were. So did national boundaries, and human nature, and so forth. If Haber had suggested that he dream up a nobler race of men, he had failed to do so.

But Haber was learning how to run his dreams better. These last two sessions had changed things quite radically. He still had his flat on Corbett Avenue, the same three rooms, faintly scented with the manager's marijuana; but he worked as a bureaucrat in a huge building downtown, and downtown was changed out of all recognition. It was almost as impressive and skyscraping as it had been when there had been no population crash, and it was much more durable and handsome. Things were being managed very differently, now.

Curiously enough, Albert M. Merdle was still President of the United States. He, like the shapes of continents, appeared to be unchangeable. But the United States was not the power it had been, nor was any single country.

Portland was now the home of the World Planning Center, the chief agency of the supranational Federation of Peoples. Portland was, as the souvenir post cards said, the Capital of the Planet. Its population was two million. The whole downtown area was full of giant WPC buildings, none more than twelve years old, all carefully planned, surrounded by green parks and tree-lined malls. Thousands of people, most of them Fed-peep or WPC employees, filled those malls; parties of tourists from Ulan Bator and Santiago de Chile filed past, heads tilted back, listening to their ear-button guides. It was a lively and imposing spectacle—the great, handsome buildings, the tended lawns, the well-dressed crowds. It looked, to George Orr, quite futuristic.

He could not find Dave's, of course. He couldn't even find Ankeny Street. He remembered it so vividly from so many other existences that he refused to accept, until he got there, the assurances of his present memory, which simply lacked any Ankeny Street at all. Where it should have been, the Research and Development Coordination Building shot cloudward from among its lawns and rhododendrons. He did not even bother to look for the Pendleton Building; Morrison Street was still there, a broad mall newly planted down the center with orange trees, but there were no neo-Inca style buildings along it, and never had been.

He could not recall the name of Heather's firm exactly; was it Forman, Esserbeck, and Rutti, or was it Forman, Esserbeck, Goodhue and Rutti? He found a telephone booth and looked for the firm. Nothing of the kind was listed, but there was a P. Esserbeck, attorney. He called there and inquired, but no Miss Lelache worked there. At last he got up his courage and looked for her name. There was no Lelache in the book.

She might still be, but bear a different name, he thought. Her mother might have dropped the husband's name after he went off to Africa. Or she might have retained her own married name after she was widowed. But he had not the least idea what her husband's name had been. She might never have borne it; many women no longer changed their names at marriage, holding the custom a relic of feminine serfdom. But what was the good of such speculations? It might very well be that there was no Heather Lelache: that—this time—she had never been born.

After facing this, Orr faced another possibility. If she walked by right now looking for me, he thought, would I recognize her?

She was brown. A clear, dark, amber brown, like Baltic amber, or a cup of strong Ceylon tea. But no brown people went by. No black people, no white, no yellow, no red.

125

They came from every part of the earth to work at the World Planning Center or to look at it, from Thailand, Argentina, Ghana, China, Ireland, Tasmania, Lebanon, Ethiopia, Vietnam, Honduras, Lichtenstein. But they all wore the same clothes, trousers, tunic, raincape; and underneath the clothes they were all the same color. They were gray.

Dr. Haber had been delighted when that happened. It had been last Saturday, their first session in a week. He had stared at himself in the washroom mirror for five minutes, chuckling and admiring; he had stared at Orr the same way. "That time you did it the economical way for once, George! By God, I believe your brain's beginning to cooperate with me! You know what I suggested you dream—eh?"

For, these days, Haber did talk freely and fully to Orr about what he was doing and hoped to do with Orr's dreams. Not that it helped much.

Orr had looked down at his own pale-gray hands, with their short gray nails. "I suppose that you suggested that there be no more color problems. No question of race."

"Precisely. And of course I was envisaging a political and ethical solution. Instead of which, your primary thinking processes took the usual short cut, which usually turns out to be a short circuit, but this time they went to the root. Made the change biological and absolute. There never has been a racial problem! You and I are the only two men on earth, George, who know that there ever was a racial problem! Can you conceive of that? Nobody was ever outcaste in India—nobody was ever lynched in Alabama—nobody was massacred in Johannesburg! War's a problem we've outgrown and race is a problem we never even had! Nobody in the entire history of the human race has suffered for the color of his skin. You're learning, George! You'll be the greatest benefactor humanity has ever had in spite of yourself. All the time and energy humans have wasted on trying to find religious solutions to suffering, then you come along and make Buddha and Jesus and the rest of them look like the fakirs they were.

They tried to run away from evil, but we, we're uprooting it—getting rid of it, piece by piece!"

Haber's paeans of triumph made Orr uneasy, and he didn't listen to them; instead, he had searched his memory and had found in it no address that had been delivered on a battlefield in Gettysburg, nor any man known to history named Martin Luther King. But such matters seemed a small price to pay for the complete retroactive abolition of racial prejudice, and he had said nothing.

But now, never to have known a woman with brown skin, brown skin and wiry black hair cut very short so that the elegant line of the skull showed like the curve of a bronze vase—no, that was wrong. That was intolerable. That every soul on earth should have a body the color of a battleship: no!

That's why she's not here, he thought. She could not have been born gray. Her color, her color of brown, was an essential part of her, not an accident. Her anger, timidity, brashness, gentleness, all were elements of her mixed being, her mixed nature, dark and clear right through, like Baltic amber. She could not exist in the gray people's world. She had not been born.

He had, though. He could be born into any world. He had no character. He was a lump of clay, a block of uncarved wood.

And Dr. Haber: he had been born. Nothing could prevent him. He only got bigger at every reincarnation.

During that terrifying day's journey from the cabin to embattled Portland, when they were bumping over a country road in the wheezing Hertz Steamer, Heather had told him that she had tried to suggest that he dream an improved Haber, as they had agreed. And since then Haber had at least been candid with Orr about his manipulations. Though candid was not the right word; Haber was much too complex a person for candor. Layer after layer might peel off the onion and yet nothing be revealed but more onion.

That peeling off of one layer was the only real change in him, and it might not be due to an effective dream, but only to changed circumstances. He was so sure of himself

127

now that he had no need to try to hide his purposes, or deceive Orr; he could simply coerce him. Orr had less chance than ever of getting away from him. Voluntary Therapeutic Treatment was now known as Personal Welfare Control, but it had the same legal teeth in it, and no lawyer would dream of bringing a patient's complaint against William Haber. He was an important man, an extremely important man. He was the Director of HURAD, the vital center of the World Planning Center, the place where the great decisions were made. He had always wanted power to do good. Now he had it.

In this light, he had remained completely true to the man Orr had first met, jovial and remote, in the dingy office in Willamette East Tower under the mural photograph of Mount Hood. He had not changed; he had simply grown.

The quality of the will to power is, precisely, growth. Achievement is its cancellation. To be, the will to power must increase with each fulfillment, making the fulfillment only a step to a further one. The vaster the power gained, the vaster the appetite for more. As there was no visible limit to the power Haber wielded through Orr's dreams, so there was no end to his determination to improve the world.

A passing Alien jostled Orr slightly in the crowd on Morrison Mall, and apologized tonelessly from its raised left elbow. The Aliens had soon learned not to point at people, finding it dismayed them. Orr looked up, startled; he had almost forgotten about the Aliens, ever since the crisis on April Fools' Day.

In the present state of affairs—or continuum, as Haber persisted in calling it—he now recalled, the Alien landing had been less of a disaster for Oregon, NASA, and the Air Force. Instead of inventing their translator-computers hastily under a rain of bombs and napalm, they had brought them with them from the Moon, and had flown about before they landed, broadcasting their peaceful intention, apologizing for the War in Space, which had all been a mistake, and asking for instructions. There had been alarm, of course, but no panic. It had been almost
128

touching to hear the toneless voices, on every band of the radio and every TV channel, repeating that the destruction of the Moondome and the Russian orbiting station had been unintended results of their ignorant efforts to make contact, that they had understood the missiles of the Space Fleet of Earth to be our own ignorant efforts to make contact, that they were very sorry and, now that they had finally mastered human channels of communication, such as speech, they wished to try to make amends.

The WPC, established in Portland since the end of the Plague Years, had coped with them, and had kept the populace and the Generals calm. This had, Orr now realized when he thought about it, not happened on the first of April a couple of weeks ago, but last year in February—fourteen months ago. The Aliens had been permitted to land; satisfactory relations with them had been established; and they had at last been allowed to leave their carefully guarded landing site near Steens Mountain in the Oregon desert and mix with men. A few of them now shared the rebuilt Moondome peacefully with Fed-peep scientists, and a couple of thousand of them were down on Earth. That was all of them that existed or, at least, all of them that had come; very few such details were released to the general public. Natives of a methane-atmosphere planet of the star Aldebaran, they had to wear their outlandish turtle-like suits perpetually on Earth or the Moon, but they didn't seem to mind. What they actually looked like, inside the turtle suits, was not clear in Orr's mind. They couldn't come out, and they didn't draw pictures. Indeed, their communication with human beings, limited to speech emission from the left elbow and some kind of auditory receiver, was limited; he was not even sure that they could see, that they had any sense organ for the visible spectrum. There were vast areas over which no communication was possible: the dolphin problem, only enormously more difficult. However, their unaggressiveness having been accepted by the WPC, and the modesty of their numbers and their aims being apparent, they had been received with a certain eagerness into Terran society. It was pleasant to have somebody different to

129

look at. They seemed to intend to stay, if allowed; some of them had already settled down to running small businesses, for they seemed to be good at salesmanship and organization, as well as space flight, their superior knowledge of which they had at once shared with Terran scientists. They had not yet made clear what they hoped for in return, why they had come to Earth. They seemed simply to like it here. As they went on behaving as industrious, peaceable, and law-abiding citizens of Earth, rumors of "Alien take-overs" and "nonhuman infiltration" had become the property of paranoid politicians of dying Nationalist splinter groups and those persons who had conversations with the *real* Flying Saucer People.

The only thing left of that terrible first of April, in fact, seemed to be the return of Mount Hood to active-volcano status. No bomb had hit it, for no bombs had fallen, this time. It had simply waked up. A long, gray-brown plume of smoke drifted northward from it now. Zigzag and Rhododendron had gone the way of Pompeii and Herculaneum. A fumarole had opened up recently near the tiny, old crater in Mount Tabor Park, well within the city limts. People in the Mount Tabor area were moving out to the thriving new suburbs of West Eastmont, Chestnut Hills Estates, and Sunny Slopes Subdivision. They could live with Mount Hood fuming softly on the horizon, but an eruption just up the street was too much.

Orr bought a tasteless plateful of fish and chips with African peanut sauce at a crowded counter-restaurant; while he ate it he thought sorrowfully, well, once I stood her up at Dave's, and now she's stood me up.

He could not face his grief, his bereavement. Dream-grief. The loss of a woman who had never existed. He tried to taste his food, to watch other people. But the food had no taste and the people were all gray.

Outside the glass doors of the restaurant the crowds were thickening: people streaming toward the Portland Palace of Sport, a huge and lavish coliseum down on the river, for the afternoon show. People didn't sit home and watch TV much any more; Fed-peep television was on only two hours a day. The modern way of life was togetherness. This was Thursday; it would be the hand-to-hands, the biggest attraction of the week except for Saturday night football. More athletes actually got killed in the hand-to-hands, but they lacked the dramatic, cathartic aspects of football, the sheer carnage when 144 men were involved at once, the drenching of the arena stands with blood. The skill of the single fighters was fine, but lacked the splendid abreactive release of mass killing.

No more war, Orr said to himself, giving up on the last soggy splinters of potato. He went out into the crowd. Ain't gonna . . . war no more. . . . There had been a song. Once. An old song. Ain't gonna . . . What was the verb? Not fight, it didn't scan. Ain't gonna . . . war no more . . . .

He walked straight into a Citizen's Arrest. A tall man with a long, wrinkled, gray face seized a short man with a round, shiny, gray face, grabbing him by the front of his tunic. The crowd bumped around the pair, some stopping to watch, others pressing on toward the Palace of Sport. "This is a Citizen's Arrest, passersby please take notice!" the tall man was saying in a piercing, nervous tenor. "This man, Harvey T. Gonno, is ill with an incurable malignant abdominal cancer but has concealed his whereabouts from the authorities and continues to live with his wife. My name is Ernest Ringo Marin, of 2624287 South West Eastwood Drive, Sunny Slopes Subdivision, Greater Portland. Are there ten witnesses?" One of the witnesses helped hold the feebly struggling criminal, while Ernest Ringo Marin counted heads. Orr escaped, pushing head-down through the crowd, before Marin administered euthanasia with the hypodermic gun worn by all adult citizens who had earned their Civic Responsibility Certificate. He himself wore one. It was a legal obligation. His, at the moment, was not loaded; its charge had been removed when he became a psychiatric patient under PWC; but they had left him the weapon so that his temporary lapse of status should not be a public humiliation to him. A mental illness such as he was being treated for, they had explained to him, must not be confused with a punishable crime such as a serious communicable or hereditary disease. He was not to feel that he was in any way a danger

131

to the Race or a second-class citizen, and his weapon would be reloaded as soon as Dr. Haber discharged him as cured.

A tumor, a tumor . . . Hadn't the carcinomic Plague, by killing off all those liable to cancer, either during the Crash or at infancy, left the survivors free of the scourge? It had, in another dream. Not in this one. Cancer had evidently broken out again, like Mount Tabor and Mount Hood.

Study. That's it. Ain't gonna study war no more. . . .

He got onto the funicular at Fourth and Alder; and swooped up over the gray-green city to the HURAD Tower which crowned the west hills, on the site of the old Pittock mansion high in Washington Park.

It overlooked everything—the city, the rivers, the hazy valleys westward, the great dark hills of Forest Park stretching north. Over the pillared portico, incised in white concrete in the straight Roman capitals whose proportions lend nobility to any phrase whatsoever, was the legend: THE GREATEST GOOD FOR THE GREATEST NUMBER.

Indoors the immense black-marble foyer, modeled after the Pantheon in Rome, bore a smaller inscription picked out in gold around the drum of the central dome: THE PROPER STUDY OF MANKIND IS MAN· A. POPE· 1688· 1744.

The building was larger in ground area, Orr had been told, than the British Museum, and five stories taller. It was also earthquake-proof. It was not bombproof, for there were no bombs. What nuclear stockpiles remained after the Cislunar War had been taken off and exploded in a series of interesting experiments out in the Asteroid Belt. This building could stand up to anything left on Earth, except perhaps Mount Hood. Or a bad dream.

He took the walkbelt to the West Wing, and the broad helical escalator to the top floor.

Dr. Haber still kept his analyst's couch in his office, a kind of ostentatiously humble reminder of his beginnings as a private practitioner, when he dealt with people by ones not by millions. But it took a while to get to the couch, for his suite covered about half an acre and included seven different rooms. Orr announced himself to the autoreceptionist at the door of the waiting room, then went on past Miss Crouch, who was feeding her computer, and past the official office, a stately room just lacking a throne, where the Director received ambassadors, delegations, and Nobel Prize winners, until at last he came to the smaller office with the wall-to-ceiling window, and the couch. There the antique redwood planels of one entire wall were slid back, exposing a magnificent array of research machinery: Haber was halfway into the exposed entrails of the Augmentor. "Hullo, George!" he boomed from within, not looking around. "Just hooking a new ergismatch into Baby's hormocouple. Half a mo. I think we'll have a session without hypnosis today. Sit down, I'll be a while at this, I've been doing a bit of tinkering again. . . . Listen. You remember that battery of tests they gave you, when you first showed up down at the Med School? Personality inventories, IQ, Rorschach, and so on and so on. Then I gave you the TAT and some simulated encounter situations, about your third session here. Remember? Ever wonder how you did on 'em?"

Haber's face, gray, framed by curly black hair and beard, appeared suddenly above the pulled-out chassis of the Augmentor. His eyes, as he gazed at Orr, reflected the light of the wall-sized window.

"I guess so," Orr said; actually he had never given it a thought.

"I believe it's time for you to know that, within the frame of reference of those standardized but extremely subtle and useful tests, you are so sane as to be an anomaly. Of course, I'm using the lay word 'sane,' which has no precise objective meaning; in quantifiable terms, you're median. Your extraversion/introversion score, for instance, was 49.1. That is, you're more introverted than extraverted by .9 of a degree. That's not unusual; what is, is the emergence of the same damn pattern everywhere, right across the board. If you put them all onto the same graph you sit smack in the middle at 50. Dominance, for example; I think you were 48.8 on that. Neither dominant nor submissive. Independence/dependence—same thing.

133

Creative/destructive, on the Ramirez scale—same thing. Both, neither. Either, or. Where there's an opposed pair, a polarity, you're in the middle; where there's a scale, you're at the balance point. You cancel out so thoroughly that, in a sense, nothing is left. Now, Walters down at the Med School reads the results a bit differently; he says your lack of social achievement is a result of your holistic adjustment, whatever that is, and that what I see as self-cancellation is a peculiar state of poise, of self-harmony. By which you can see that, let's face it, old Walters is a pious fraud, he's never outgrown the mysticism of the seventies; but he means well. So there you have it, anyway: you're the man in the middle of the graph. There we are, now to hook up the glumdalclitch with the brobdingnag, and we're all set. . . . Hell!" He had knocked his head on a panel getting up. He left the Augmentor open. "Well, you're a queer fish, George, and the queerest thing about you is that there's nothing queer about you!" He laughed his huge, gusty laugh. "So, today we try a new tack. No hypnosis. No sleep. No d-state and no dreams. Today I want to hook you up with the Augmentor in a waking state."

Orr's heart sank, though he did not know why. "What for?" he said.

"Principally to get a record of your normal waking brain rhythms when augmented. I got a full analysis your first session, but that was before the Augmentor could do anything but fall in with the rhythm you were currently emitting. Now I'll be able to use it to stimulate and trace certain individual characteristics of your brain activity more clearly, particularly that tracer-shell effect you have in the hippocampus. Then I can compare them with your d-state patterns, and with the patterns of other brains, normal and abnormal. I'm looking for what makes you tick, George, so that I can find what makes your dreams work."

"What for?" Orr repeated.

"What for? Well, isn't that what you're here for?"

"I came here to be cured. To learn how *not* to dream effectively."

134

"If you'd been a simple one-two-three cure, would you have been sent up here to the Institute, to HURAD—to me?"

Orr put his head in his hands, and said nothing.

"I can't show you how to stop, George, until I can find out what it is you're doing."

"But if you do find out, will you tell me how to stop?"

Haber rocked back largely on his heels. "Why are you so afraid of yourself, George?"

"I'm not," Orr said. His hands were sweaty. "I'm afraid of—" But he was too afraid, in fact, to say the pronoun.

"Of changing things, as you call it. O.K. I know. We've been through that many times. *Why*, George? You've got to ask yourself that question. What's wrong with changing things? Now, I wonder if this self-canceling, centerpoised personality of yours leads you to look at things defensively. I want you to try to detach yourself from yourself and try to see your own viewpoint from the outside, objectively. You are afraid of *losing your balance*. But change need not unbalance you; life's not a static object, after all. It's a process. There's no holding still. Intellectually you know that, but emotionally you refuse it. Nothing remains the same from one moment to the next, you can't step into the same river twice. Life—evolution—the whole universe of space/time, matter/energy—existence itself—is essentially *change*."

"That is one aspect of it," Orr said. "The other is stillness."

"When things don't change any longer, that's the end result of entropy, the heat-death of the universe. The more things go on moving, interrelating, conflicting, changing, the less balance there is—and the more life. I'm pro-life, George. Life itself is a huge gamble against the odds, against all odds! You can't try to live safely, there's no such thing as safety. Stick your neck out of your shell, then, and live *fully!* It's not how you get there, but where you get to that counts. What you're afraid to accept, here, is that we're engaged in a really great experiment, you and I. We're on the brink of discovering and controlling, for the good of all mankind, a whole new force, an entire new

135

field of antientropic energy, of the life-force, of the will to act, to do, to change!"

"All that is true. But there is—"

"What, George?" He was fatherly and patient, now; and Orr forced himself to go on, knowing it was no good.

"We're in the world, not against it. It doesn't work to try to stand outside things and run them, that way. It just doesn't work, it goes against life. There is a way but you have to follow it. The world *is*, no matter how we think it ought to be. You have to be with it. You have to let it be."

Haber walked up and down the room, pausing before the huge window that framed a view northward of the serene and nonerupting cone of Mount St. Helen. He nodded several times. "I understand," he said with his back turned. "I understand completely. But let me put it this way, George, and perhaps you'll understand what it is I'm after. You're alone in the jungle, in the Mato Grosso, and you find a native woman lying on the path, dying of snakebite. You have serum in your kit, plenty of it, enough to cure thousands of snakebites. Do you withhold it because 'this is the way it is'—do you 'let her be'?"

"It would depend," Orr said.

"Depend on *what?*"

"Well . . . I don't know. If reincarnation is a fact, you might be keeping her from a better life and condemning her to live out a wretched one. Perhaps you cure her and she goes home and murders six people in the village. I know you'd give her the serum, because you have it, and feel sorry for her. But you don't know whether what you're doing is good or evil or both. . . ."

"O.K.! Granted! I know what snakebite serum does, but I don't know what I'm doing—O.K., I'll buy it on those terms, gladly. And say what's the difference? I freely admit that I don't know, about 85 per cent of the time, what the hell I'm doing with this screwball brain of yours, and you don't either, but we're *doing* it—so, can we get on with it?" His virile, genial vigor was overwhelming; he laughed, and Orr found a weak smile on his lips.

While the electrodes were being applied, however, he made one last effort to communicate with Haber. "I saw a

Citizen's Arrest for euthanasia on the way here," he said.

"What for?"

"Eugenics. Cancer."

Haber nodded, alert. "No wonder you're depressed. You haven't yet fully accepted the use of controlled violence for the good of the community; you may never be able to. This is a tough-minded world we've got going here, George. A realistic one. But as I said, life can't be safe. This society is tough-minded, and getting tougher yearly: the future will justify it. We need health. We simply have no room for the incurables, the gene-damaged who degrade the species; we have no time for wasted, useless suffering." He spoke with an enthusiasm that rang hollower than usual; Orr wondered how well, in fact, Haber liked this world he had indubitably made. "Now just sit like that, I don't want you going to sleep from force of habit. O.K., great. You may get bored. I want you just to sit for a while. Keep your eyes open, think about anything you like. I'll be fiddling with Baby's guts, here. Now, here we go: bingo." He pressed the white ON button in the wall panel to the right of the Augmentor, by the head of the couch.

A passing Alien jostled Orr slightly in the crowd on the mall; it raised its left elbow to apologize, and Orr muttered, "Sorry." It stopped, half blocking his way: and he too halted, startled and impressed by its nine-foot, greenish, armored impassivity. It was grotesque to the point of being funny; like a sea turtle, and yet like a sea turtle it possessed a strange, large beauty, a serener beauty than that of any dweller in sunlight, any walker on the earth.

From the still-lifted left elbow the voice issued flatly: "Jor Jor," it said.

After a moment Orr recognized his own name in this Barsoomian bisyllable, and said with some embarrassment, "Yes, I'm Orr."

"Please forgive warranted interruption. You are human capable of *iahklu'* as previously noted. This troubles self."

"I don't—I think—"

"We also have been variously disturbed. Concepts cross in mist. Perception is difficult. Volcanoes emit fire. Help is

137

offered: refusably. Snakebite serum is not prescribed for all. Before following directions leading in wrong directions, auxiliary forces may be summoned, in immediate-following fashion: *Er' perrehnne!"*

"*Er' perrehnne,"* Orr repeated automatically, his whole mind intent on trying to understand what the Alien was telling him.

"If desired. Speech is silver, silence is gold. Self is universe. Please forgive interruption, crossing in mist." The Alien, though neckless and waistless, gave an impression of bowing, and passed on, huge and greenish above the gray-faced crowd. Orr stood staring after him until Haber said, "George!"

"What?" He looked stupidly around at the room, the desk, the window.

"What the hell did you do?"

"Nothing," Orr said. He was still sitting on the couch, his hair full of electrodes. Haber had pushed the OFF button of the Augmentor and had come around in front of the couch, staring first at Orr and then at the EEG screen.

He opened the machine and checked the permanent record inside it, recorded by pens on paper tape. "Thought I'd misread the screen," he said, and gave a peculiar laugh, a very clipped version of his usual full-throated roar. "Queer stuff going on in your cortex there, and I wasn't even feeding your cortex at all with the Augmentor, I'd just begun a slight stimulus to the pons, nothing specific. . . . What's this. . . . Christ, that must be 150 mv there." He turned suddenly to Orr. "What were you thinking? Reconstruct it."

An extreme reluctance possessed Orr, amounting to a sense of threat, of danger.

"I thought—I was thinking about the Aliens."

"The Aldebaranians? Well?"

"I just thought of one I saw on the street, coming here."

"And that reminded you, consciously or unconsciously, of the euthanasia you saw performed. Right? O.K. That might explain the funny business here down in the emotive centers, the Augmentor picked it up and exaggerated it.

138

You must have felt that—something special, unusual going on in your mind?"

"No," Orr said, truthfully. It had not *felt* unusual.

"O.K. Now look, in case my reactions worried you there, you should know that I've had this Augmentor hooked up to my own brain several hundred times, and on lab subjects, some forty-five different subjects in fact. It's not going to hurt you any more than it did them. But that reading was a very unusual one for an adult subject, and I simply wanted to check with you to see if you felt it subjectively."

Haber was reassuring himself, not Orr; but it didn't matter. Orr was past reassurance.

"O.K. Here we go again." Haber restarted the EEG, and approached the ON button of the Augmentor. Orr set his teeth and faced Chaos and Old Night.

But they were not there. Nor was he downtown talking to a nine-foot turtle. He remained sitting on the comfortable couch looking at the misty, blue-gray cone of St. Helen out the window. And, quiet as a thief in the night, a sense of well-being came into him, a certainty that things were all right, and that he was in the middle of things. Self is universe. He would not be allowed to be isolated, to be stranded. He was back where he belonged. He felt an equanimity, a perfect certainty as to where he was and where everything else was. This feeling did not come to him as blissful or mystical, but simply as normal. It was the way he generally had felt, except in times of crisis, of agony; it was the mood of his childhood and all the best and profoundest hours of the boyhood and maturity; it was his natural mode of being. These last years he had lost it, gradually but almost entirely, scarcely realizing that he had lost it. Four years ago this month, four years ago in April, something had happened that had made him lose that balance altogether for a while; and recently the drugs he had taken, the dreams he had dreamed, the constant jumping from one life-memory to another, the worsening of the texture of life the more Haber improved it, all this had sent him clear off course. Now, all at once, he was back where he belonged.

He knew that this was nothing he had accomplished by himself.

He said aloud, "Did the Augmentor do that?"

"Do what?" said Haber, leaning around the machinery again to watch the EEG screen.

"Oh . . . I don't know."

"It isn't doing anything, in your sense," Haber replied with a touch of irritation. Haber was likable at moments like this, playing no role and pretending no response, wholly absorbed in what he was trying to learn from the quick and subtle reactions of his machines. "It's merely amplifying what your own brain's doing at the moment, selectively reinforcing the activity, and your brain's doing absolutely nothing interesting. . . . There." He made a rapid note of something, returned to the Augmentor, then leaned back to observe the jiggling lines on the little screen. He separated three that had seemed one, by turning dials, then reunified them. Orr did not interrupt him again. Once Haber said sharply, "Shut your eyes. Roll the eyeballs upward. Right. Keep them shut, try to visualize something—a red cube. Right . . . ."

When at last he turned the machines off and began to detach the electrodes, the serenity Orr had felt did not lapse, like the induced mood of a drug or alcohol. It remained. Without premeditation and without timidity Orr said, "Dr. Haber, I can't let you use my effective dreams any more."

"Eh?" Haber said, his mind still on Orr's brain, not on Orr.

"I can't let you use my dreams any more."

" 'Use' them?"

"Use them."

"Call it what you like," Haber said. He had straightened up and towered over Orr, who was still sitting down. He was gray, large, broad, curly bearded, deep-chested, frowning. Your God is a jealous God. "I'm sorry, George, but you're not in a position to say that."

Orr's gods were nameless and unenvious, asking neither worship nor obedience.

"Yet I do say it," he replied mildly.

140

Haber looked down at him, really looked at him for a moment, and saw him. He seemed to recoil, as a man might who thought to push aside a gauze curtain and found it to be a granite door. He crossed the room. He sat down behind his desk. Orr now stood up and stretched a little.

Haber stroked his black beard with a big, gray hand.

"I am on the verge—no, I'm in the midst—of a breakthrough," he said, his deep voice not booming or jovial but dark, powerful. "Using your brain patterns in a feedback-elimination-replication-augmentation routine, I am programming the Augmentor to reproduce the EEG rhythms that obtain during effective dreaming. I call these e-state rhythms. When I have them sufficiently generalized, I will be able to superimpose them on the d-state rhythms of another brain, and after a period of synchronization they will, I believe, induce effective dreaming in that brain. Do you understand what that means? I'll be able to induce the e-state in a properly selected and trained brain, as easily as a psychologist using ESB induces rage in a cat, or tranquillity in a psychotic human—more easily, for I can stimulate without implanting contacts or chemicals. I am within a few days, perhaps a few hours, of accomplishing this goal. Once I do, you're off the hook. You will be unnecessary. I don't like working with an unwilling subject, and progress will be much faster with a suitably equipped and oriented subject. But until I'm ready, I need you. This research must be finished. It is probably the most important piece of scientific research that has ever been done. I need you to the extent that—if your sense of obligation to me as a friend, and to the pursuit of knowledge, and to the welfare of all humanity, isn't sufficient to keep you here—then I'm willing to compel you to serve a higher cause. If necessary, I'll obtain an order of Obligatory Ther— of Personal Welfare Constraint. If necessary, I'll use drugs, as if you were a violent psychotic. Your refusal to help in a matter of this importance is, of course, psychotic. Needless to say, however, I would infinitely rather have your free, voluntary help, without legal or psychic coercion. It would make all the difference to me."

141

"It really wouldn't make any difference to you," Orr said, without belligerence.

"Why are you fighting me—now? Why now, George? When you've contributed so much, and we're so near the goal?" Your God is a reproachful God. But guilt was not the way to get at George Orr; if he had been a man much given to guilt feelings he would not have lived to thirty.

"Because the longer you go on the worse it gets. And now, instead of preventing me from having effective dreams, you're going to start having them yourself. I don't like making the rest of the world live in my dreams, but I certainly don't want to live in yours."

"What do you mean by that: 'the worse it gets'? Look here, George." Man to man. Reason will prevail. If only we sit down and talk things over. . . . "In the few weeks that we've worked together, this is what we've done. Eliminated overpopulation; restored the quality of urban life and the ecological balance of the planet. Eliminated cancer as a major killer." He began to bend his strong, gray fingers down, enumerating. "Eliminated the color problem, racial hatred. Eliminated war. Eliminated the risk of species deterioration and the fostering of deleterious gene stocks. Eliminated—no, say in process of eliminating—poverty, economic inequality, the class war, all over the world. What else? Mental illness, maladjustment to reality: that'll take a while, but we've made the first steps already. Under HURAD direction, the reduction of human misery, physical and psychic, and the constant increase of valid individual self-expression, is an ongoing thing, a constant progress. Progress, George! We've made more progress in six weeks than humanity made in six hundred thousand years!"

Orr felt that all these arguments should be answered. He began, "But where's democratic government got to? People can't choose anything at all any more for themselves. Why is everything so shoddy, why is everybody so joyless? You can't even tell people apart—and the younger they are the more that's so. This business of World State bringing up all the children in those Centers—"

142

But Haber interrupted, really angry. "The Child Centers were your invention, not mine! I simply outlined the desiderata to you among the suggestions for a dream, as I always do; I tried to suggest how to implement some of them, but those suggestions never seem to take hold, or they get twisted out of all recognition by your damned primary-process thinking. You don't have to tell me that you resist and resent everything I'm trying to accomplish for humanity, you know—that's been obvious from the start. Every step forward that I force you to take, you cancel, you cripple with the deviousness or stupidity of the means your dream takes to realize it. You try, each time, to take a step backward. Your own drives are totally negative. If you weren't under strong hypnotic compulsion when you dream, you'd have reduced the world to ashes, weeks ago! Look what you almost did, that one night when you ran off with that woman lawyer—"

"She's dead," Orr said.

"Good. She was a destructive influence on you. Irresponsible. You have no social conscience, no altruism. You're a moral jellyfish. I have to instill social responsibility in you hypnotically, every time. And every time it's thwarted, spoiled. That's what happened with the Child Centers. I suggested that the nuclear family being the prime shaper of neurotic personality structures, there were certain ways in which it might, in an ideal society, be modified. Your dream simply grabbed at the crudest interpretation of these, mixed it up with cheap utopian concepts, or cynical anti-utopian concepts perhaps, and produced the Centers. Which, all the same, are better than what they replaced! There is very little schizophrenia in this world—did you know that? It's a rare disease!" Haber's dark eyes shone, his lips grinned.

"Things are better than they—than they were once," Orr said, abandoning hope of discussion. "But as you go on they get worse. I'm not trying to thwart you, it's that you're trying to do something that can't be done. I have this, this gift, I know that; and I know my obligation to it. To use it only when I must. When there is no other alternative. There *are* alternatives now. I've got to stop."

143

"We can't stop—we've just begun! We're just beginning to get any control at all over this power of yours. I'm within sight of doing so, and I will do so. No personal fears can stand in the way of the good that can be done for all men with this new capacity of the human brain!"

Haber was speechmaking. Orr looked at him, but the opaque eyes, gazing straight at him, did not return his look, did not see him. The speech went on.

"What I'm doing is making this new capacity *replicable*. There's an analogy with the invention of printing, with the application of any new technological or scientific concept. If the experiment or technique cannot be repeated successfully by others, it is of no use. Similarly, the e-state, so long as it was locked into the brain of a single man, was no more use to humanity than a key locked inside a room, or a single, sterile genius mutation. But I'll have the means of getting the key out of that room. And that 'key' will be as great a milestone in human evolution as the development of the reasoning brain itself! Any brain capable of using it, deserving of using it, will be able to. When a suitable, trained, prepared subject enters the e-state under the Augmentor stimulus, he will be under complete autohypnotic control. Nothing will be left to chance, to random impulse, to irrational narcissistic whim. There will be none of this tension between your will to nihilism and my will to progress, your Nirvana wishes and my conscious, careful planning for the good of all. When I have made sure of my techniques, then you'll be free to go. Absolutely free. And since you've claimed all along that all you want is to be free of responsibility, incapable of dreaming effectively, then I'll promise that my very first effective dream will include your 'cure'—you'll never have an effective dream again."

Orr had risen; he stood still, looking at Haber; his face was calm but intensely alert and centered. "You will control your own dreams," he said, "by yourself—no one helping, or supervising you—?"

"I've controlled yours for weeks now. In my own case, and of course I'll be the first subject of my own experiment, that's an absolute ethical obligation, in my own case the control will be complete."

"I tried autohypnosis, before I ever used the dream-suppressing drugs—"

"Yes, you mentioned that before; you failed, of course. The question of a resistant subject achieving successful autosuggestion is an interesting one, but this was no test of it whatever; you're not a professional psychologist, you're not a trained hypnotist, and you were already emotionally disturbed about the whole issue; you got nowhere, of course. But I *am* a professional, and I know precisely what I'm doing. I can autosuggest an entire dream and dream it in every detail precisely as thought out by my waking mind. I've done so, every night this past week, getting in training. When the Augmentor synchronizes the generalized e-state pattern with my own d-state, such dreams will be effectivized. And then—and then—" The lips within the curly beard parted in a straining, staring smile, a grin of ecstasy that made Orr turn away as if he had seen something never meant to be seen, both terrifying and pathetic. "Then this world will be like heaven, and men will be like gods!"

"We are, we are already," Orr said, but the other paid no heed.

"There is nothing to fear. The dangerous time—had we known it—was when you alone possessed the capacity for e-dreaming, and didn't know what to do with it. If you hadn't come to me, if you hadn't been sent into trained, scientific hands, who knows what might have happened. But you were here, and I was here: as they say, genius consists in being in the right time in the right place!" He boomed a laugh. "So now there's nothing to fear, and it's all out of your hands. I know, scientifically and morally, what I'm doing and how to do it. I know where I'm going."

"Volcanoes emit fire," Orr murmured.

"What? "

"May I go now?"

"Tomorrow at five."

"I'll come," Orr said, and left.

10

Il descend, réveillé, l'autre côté du rêve.
—Hugo, *Contemplations*

It was only three o'clock, and he should have gone back to his office in the Parks Department and finished up the plans for southeast suburban play areas; but he didn't. He gave it one thought and dismissed it. Although his memory assured him that he had held that position for five years now, he disbelieved his memory; the job had no reality to him. It was not work he had to do. It was not his job.

He was aware that in thus relegating to irreality a major portion of the only reality, the only existence, that he in fact did have, he was running exactly the same risk the insane mind runs: the loss of the sense of free will. He knew that in so far as one denies what is, one is possessed by what is not, the compulsions, the fantasies, the terrors that flock to fill the void. But the void was there. This life lacked realness; it was hollow; the dream, creating where there was no necessity to create, had worn thin and sleazy. If this was being, perhaps the void was better. He would accept the monsters and the necessities beyond reason. He would go home, and take no drugs, but sleep, and dream what dreams might come.

He got off the funicular downtown, but instead of taking the trolley he set out walking toward his own district; he had always liked to walk.

Along past Lovejoy Park a piece of the old freeway was still standing, a huge ramp, probably dating from the last frenetic convulsions of highway-mania in the seventies; it must have led up to the Marquam Bridge, once, but now ended abruptly in mid-air thirty feet above Front Avenue. It had not been destroyed when the city was cleaned up and rebuilt after the Plague Years, perhaps because it was so large, so useless, and so ugly as to be, to the American eye, invisible. There it stood, and a few bushes had taken root up on the roadway, while underneath it a huddle of buildings had grown up, like swallows' nests in a cliff. In this rather dowdy and noncommittal bit of the city there were still small shops, independent markets, unappetizing little restaurants, and so on, struggling along despite the stringencies of total Consumer Product Equity-Rationing and the overwhelming competition of the great WPC Marts and Outlets, through which 90 per cent of world trade was now channeled.

One of these shops under the ramp was a secondhand store; the sign above the windows said ANTIQUES and a poorly lettered, peeling sign painted on the glass said JUNQUE. There was some squat handmade pottery in one window, an old rocker with a motheaten paisley shawl draped over it in the other, and, scattered around these main displays, all kinds of cultural litter: a horseshoe, a hand-wound clock, something enigmatic from a dairy, a framed photograph of President Eisenhower, a slightly chipped glass globe containing three Ecuadorian coins, a plastic toilet-seat cover decorated with baby crabs and seaweed, a well-thumbed rosary, and a stack of old hi-fi 45 rpm records, marked "Gd Cond," but obviously scratched. Just the sort of place, Orr thought, where Heather's mother might have worked for a while. Moved by the impulse, he went in.

It was cool and rather dark inside. A leg of the ramp formed one wall, a high blank dark expanse of concrete, like the wall of an undersea cave. From the receding prospect of shadows, bulky furniture, decrepit acres of Action Paintings and fake-antique spinning wheels now becoming genuinely antique though still useless, from these tenebrous reaches of no-man's-things, a huge form emerged, seeming to float forward slowly, silent and reptilian: The proprietor was an Alien.

147

It raised its crooked left elbow and said, "Good day. Do you wish an object?"

"Thanks, I was just looking."

"Please continue this activity," the proprietor said. It withdrew a little way into the shadows and stood quite motionless. Orr looked at the light play on some ratty old peacock feathers, observed a 1950 home-movie projector, a blue and white saki set, a heap of *Mad* magazines, priced quite high. He hefted a solid steel hammer and admired its balance; it was a well-made tool, a good thing. "Is this your own choice?" he asked the proprietor, wondering what the Aliens themselves might prize from all this flotsam of the affluent years of America.

"What comes is acceptable," the Alien replied.

A congenial point of view. "I wonder if you'd tell me something. In your language, what is the meaning of the word *iahklu'*?"

The proprietor came slowly forward again, edging the broad, shell-like armor carefully among fragile objects.

"Incommunicable. Language used for communication with individual-persons will not contain other forms of relationship. Jor Jor." The right hand, a great, greenish, flipperlike extremity, came forward in a slow and perhaps tentative fashion. "Tiua'k Ennbe Ennbe."

Orr shook hands with it. It stood immobile, apparently regarding him, though no eyes were visible inside the dark-tinted, vapor-filled headpiece. If it was a headpiece. Was there in fact any substantial form within that green carapace, that mighty armor? He didn't know. He felt, however, completely at ease with Tiua'k Ennbe Ennbe.

"I don't suppose," he said, on impulse again, "that you ever knew anyone named Lelache?"

"Lelache. No. Do you seek Lelache."

"I have lost Lelache."

"Crossings in mist," the Alien observed.

"That's about it," Orr said. He picked up from the crowded table before him a white bust of Franz Schubert about two inches high, probably a piano-teacher's prize to a pupil. On the base the pupil had written, "What, Me

148

Worry?" Schubert's face was mild and impassive, a tiny bespectacled Buddha. "How much is this?" Orr asked.

"Five New Cents," replied Tiua'k Ennbe Ennbe.

Orr produced a Fed-peep nickel.

"Is there any way to control *iahklu'*, to make it go the way it . . . ought to go?"

The Alien took the nickel and sidled majestically over to a chrome-plated cash register which Orr had assumed was for sale as an antique. It rang up the sale on the register and stood still a while.

"One swallow does not make a summer," it said. "Many hands make light work." It stopped again, apparently not satisfied with this effort at bridging the communication gap. It stood still for half a minute, then went to the front window and with precise, stiff, careful movements picked out one of the antique disk-records displayed there, and brought it to Orr. It was a Beatles record: "With a Little Help from My Friends."

"Gift," it said. "Is it acceptable?"

"Yes," Orr said, and took the record. "Thank you— thanks very much. It's very kind of you. I am grateful."

"Pleasure," said the Alien. Though the mechanically produced voice was toneless and the armor impassive, Orr was sure that Tiua'k Ennbe Ennbe was in fact pleased; he himself was moved.

"I can play this on my landlord's machine, he has an old disk-phonograph," he said. "Thank you very much." They shook hands again, and he left.

After all, he thought as he walked on toward Corbett Avenue, it's not surprising that the Aliens are on my side. In a sense, I invented them. I have no idea in what sense, of course. But they definitely weren't around until I dreamed they were, until I let them be. So that there is—there always was—a connection between us.

Of course (his thoughts proceeded, also at a walking pace), it that's true, then the whole world as it now is should be on my side; because I dreamed a lot of it up, too. Well, after all, it *is* on my side. That is, I'm a part of it. Not separate from it. I walk on the ground and the ground's walked on by me, I breathe the air and change it, I am entirely interconnected with the world.

Only Haber's different, and more different with each dream. He's against me: my connection with him is negative. And that aspect of the world which he's responsible for, which he ordered me to dream, that's what I feel alienated from, powerless against. . . .

It's not that he's evil. He's right, one ought to try to help other people. But that analogy with snakebite serum was false. He was talking about one person meeting another person in pain. That's different. Perhaps what I did, what I did in April four years ago . . . was justified. . . . (But his thoughts shied away, as always, from the burned place.) You have to help another person. But it's not right to play God with masses of people. To be God you have to know what you're doing. And to do any good at all, just believing you're right and your motives are good isn't enough. You have to . . . be in touch. He isn't in touch. No one else, no thing even, has an existence of its own for him; he sees the world only as a means to his end. It doesn't make any difference if his end is good; means are all we've got. . . . He can't accept, he can't let be, he can't let go. He is insane. . . . He could take us all with him, out of touch, if he did manage to dream as I do. What am I to do?

He reached the old house on Corbett as he reached that question.

He stopped off in the basement to borrow the old-fashioned phonograph from Mannie Ahrens, the manager. This involved sharing a pot of tea. Mannie always brewed it for Orr, since Orr had never smoked and couldn't inhale without coughing. They discussed world affairs a little. Mannie hated the Sports Shows; he stayed home and watched the WPC educational shows for pre-Child Center children every afternoon. "The alligator puppet, Dooby Doo, he's a real cool cat," he said. There were long gaps in the conversation, reflections of the large holes in the fabric of Mannie's mind, worn thin by the application of innumerable chemicals over the years. But there was peace and privacy in his grubby basement, and weak cannabis tea had

150

a mildly relaxing effect on Orr. At last he lugged the phonograph upstairs, and plugged it into a wall-socket in his bare living room. He put the record on, and then held the needle-arm suspended over the turning disk. What did he want?

He didn't know. Help, he supposed. Well, what came would be acceptable, as Tiua'k Ennbe Ennbe had said.

He set the needle carefully on the outer groove, and lay down beside the phonograph on the dusty floor.

Do you need anybody?
I need somebody to love.

The machine was automatic; when it had played the record it grumbled softly a moment, clicked its innards, and returned the needle to the first groove.

I get by, with a little help,
With a little help from my friends.

During the eleventh replay Orr fell sound asleep.

Awakening in the high, bare, twilit room, Heather was disconcerted. Where on earth?

She had been asleep. Gone to sleep sitting on the floor with her legs stretched out and her back against the piano. Marijuana always made her sleepy, and stupid, too, but you couldn't hurt Mannie's feelings and refuse it, the poor old pothead. George lay flat as a skinned cat on the floor, right by the phonograph, which was slowly eating its way through "With a Little Help" right down to the turntable. She cut the volume down slowly, then stopped the machine. George never stirred; his lips were slightly parted, his eyes firmly closed. How funny that they had both gone to sleep listening to the music. She got up off her knees and went out to the kitchen to see what was for dinner.

Oh for Christsake, pig liver. It was nourishing and the best value you could get for three meat-ration stamps by weight. She had picked it up at the Mart yesterday. Well, cut real thin, and fried with salt pork and onions . . .

151

yecchh. Oh well, she was hungry enough to eat pig liver, and George wasn't a picky man. If it was decent food he ate and enjoyed it and if it was lousy pig liver he ate it. Praise God from whom all blessings flow, including good-natured men.

As she set the kitchen table and put two potatoes and half a cabbage on to cook, she paused from time to time: she did feel odd. Disoriented. From the damn pot, and going to sleep on the floor at all hours, no doubt.

George came in, disheveled and dusty-shirted. He stared at her. She said, "Well. Good morning!"

He stood looking at her and smiling, a broad radiant smile of pure joy. She had never received so great a compliment in her life; she was abashed by that joy, which she had caused. "My dear wife," he said, taking her hands. He looked at them, palms and backs, and put them up against his face. "You should be brown," he said, and to her dismay she saw tears in his eyes. For a moment, just that moment, she had a notion of what was going on; she recalled being brown, and remembered the silence in the cabin at night, and the sound of the creek, and many other things, all in a flash. But George was a more urgent consideration. She was holding him, as he held her. "You're worn out," she said, "you're upset, you fell asleep on the floor. It's that bastard Haber. Don't go back to him. Just don't. I don't care what he does, we'll take it to court, we'll appeal it, even if he slaps a Constraint injunction on you and sticks you in Linnton we'll get you a different shrink and get you out again. You can't go on with him, he's destroying you."

"Nobody can destroy me," he said, and laughed a little, deep in his chest, almost a sob, "not so long as I have a little help from my friends. I'll go back, it's not going to last much longer. It's not me I'm worried about, any more. But don't worry...." They hung on to each other, in touch at all available surfaces, absolutely unified, while the liver and onions sizzled in the pan. "I fell asleep too," she said into his neck, "I got so groggy typing up old Rutti's dumb letters. But that's a good record you bought. I loved

152

the Beatles when I was a kid but the Government stations never play them any more."

"It was a present," George said, but the liver popped in the pan, and she had to disengage herself and see to it. At dinner George watched her; she watched him a good bit, too. They had been married seven months. They said nothing of any importance. They washed up the dishes and went to bed. In bed, they made love. Love doesn't just sit there, like a stone, it has to be made, like bread; re-made all the time, made new. When it was made, they lay in each other's arms, holding love, asleep. In her sleep Heather heard the roaring of a creek full of the voices of unborn children singing.

In his sleep George saw the depths of the open sea.

Heather was the secretary of an aged and otiose legal partnership, Ponder and Rutti. When she got off work at four-thirty the next day, Friday, she didn't take the monorail and trolley home, but rode the funicular up to Washington Park. She had told George she might come meet him at HURAD, since his therapy session wasn't till five, and after it they might go back downtown together and eat at one of the WPC restaurants on the International Mall. "It'll be all right," he told her, understanding her motive and meaning that he would be all right. She replied, "I know. But it would be fun to eat out, and I saved some stamps. We haven't tried the Casa Boliviana yet."

She got to the HURAD tower early, and waited on the vast marble steps. He came on the next car. She saw him get off, with others whom she did not see. A short, neatly made man, very self-contained, with an amiable expression. He moved well, though he stooped a little like most desk workers. When he saw her his eyes, which were clear and light, seemed to grow lighter, and he smiled: again that heartbreaking smile of unmitigated joy. She loved him violently. If Haber hurt him again she would go in there and tear Haber into little bits. Violent feelings were foreign to her, usually, but not where George was concerned. And anyhow, today for some reason she felt different from usual. She felt bolder, harder. She had said "shit" aloud, twice, at work, making old Mr. Rutti flinch. She had

153

hardly ever said "shit" before aloud, and she hadn't intended to do so either time, and yet she had done it, as if it were a habit too old to break. . . .

"Hello, George," she said.

"Hello," he said, taking her hands. "You are beautiful, beautiful."

How could anybody think this man was sick? All right, so he had funny dreams. That was better than being plain mean and hateful, like about one quarter of the people she had ever met.

"It's five already," she said. "I'll wait down here. If it rains, I'll be in the lobby. It's like Napoleon's Tomb in there, all that black marble and stuff. It's nice out here, though. You can hear the lions roaring down in the Zoo."

"Come on up with me," he said. "It's raining already." In fact it was, the endless warm drizzle of spring—the ice of Antarctica, falling softly on the heads of the children of those responsible for melting it. "He's got a nice waiting room. You'll probably be sharing it with a mess of Fedpeep bigwigs and three or four Chiefs of State. All dancing attendance on the Director of HURAD. And I have to go crawling through and get shown in ahead of them, every damn time. Dr. Haber's tame psycho. His exhibition. His token patient. . . ." He was steering her through the big lobby under the Pantheon dome, onto moving walkways, up an incredible, apparently endless, spiral escalator. "HURAD really runs the world, as is," he said. "I can't help wondering why Haber needs any other form of power. He's got enough, God knows. Why can't he stop here? I suppose it's like Alexander the Great, needing new worlds to conquer. I never did understand that. How was work today?"

He was tense, that's why he was talking so much; but he didn't seem depressed or distressed, as he had for weeks. Something had restored his natural equanimity. She had never really believed that he could lose it for long, lose his way, get out of touch; yet he had been wretched, increasingly so. Now he was not, and the change was so sudden and complete that she wondered what, in fact, had worked it. All she could date it from was their sitting down in the

154

still-unfurnished living room to listen to that nutty and subtle Beatles song last evening, and both falling asleep. From then on, he had been himself again.

Nobody was in Haber's big, sleek waiting room. George said his name to a desklike thing by the door, an auto-receptionist, he explained to Heather. She was making a nervous funny about did they have autoeroticists, too, when a door opened, and Haber stood in the doorway.

She had met him only once, and briefly, when he first took George as a patient. She had forgotten what a big man he was, how big a beard he had, how drastically impressive he looked. "Come on in, George!" he thundered. She was awed. She cowered. He noticed her. "Mrs. Orr—glad to see you! Glad you came! You come on in, too."

"Oh no. I just—"

"Oh yes. D'you realize that this is probably George's last session here? Did he tell you? Tonight we wind it up. You certainly ought to be present. Come on. I've let my staff out early. Expect you saw the stampede on the Down escalator. Felt like having the place to myself tonight. That's it, sit down there." He went on; there was no need to say anything meaningful in reply. She was fascinated by Haber's demeanor, the kind of exultation he exuded; she hadn't remembered what a masterful, genial person he was, larger than life-size. It was unbelievable, really, that such a man, a world leader and a great scientist, should have spent all these weeks of personal therapy on George, who wasn't anybody. But, of course, George's case was very important, researchwise.

"One last session," he was saying, while adjusting something in a computerish-looking thing in the wall at the head of the couch. "One last controlled dream, and then, I think, we've got the problem licked. You game, George?"

He used her husband's name often. She remembered George's saying a couple of weeks ago, "He keeps calling me by my name; I think it's to remind himself that there's someone else present."

"Sure, I'm game," George said, and sat down on the couch, lifting his face a little; he glanced once at Heather

155

and smiled. Haber at once started attaching the little things on wires to his head, parting the thick hair to do so. Heather remembered that process from her own brain-printing, part of the battery of tests and records made on every Fed-peep citizen. It made her uneasy to see it done to her husband. As if the electrode things were little suction cups that would drain the thoughts out of George's head and turn them into scribbles on a piece of paper, the meaningless writing of the mad. George's face now wore a look of extreme concentration. What was he thinking?

Haber put his hand on George's throat suddenly as if about to throttle him, and reaching out with the other hand, started a tape which spoke the hypnotist's spiel in his own voice: "You are entering the hypnotic state...." Within a few seconds he stopped it and tested for hypnosis. George was under.

"O.K.," Huber said, and paused, evidently pondering. Huge, like a grizzly bear reared up on its hind legs, he stood there between her and the slight, passive figure on the couch.

"Now listen carefully, George, and remember what I say. You are deeply hypnotized and will follow explicitly all instructions I give you. You're going to go to sleep when I tell you to, and you'll dream. You'll have an effective dream. You'll dream that you are completely normal—that you are like everybody else. You'll dream that you once had, or thought you had, a capacity for effective dreaming, but that this is *no longer true*. Your dreams from henceforth will be just like everybody else's, meaningful to you alone, having no effect on outward reality. You'll dream all this; whatever symbolism you use to express the dream, its effective content will be that you can no longer dream effectively. It will be a pleasant dream, and you'll wake up when I say your name three times, feeling alert and well. After this dream you will never dream effectively again. Now, lie back. Get comfortable. You're going to sleep. You're asleep. Antwerp!"

As he said this last word, George's lips moved and he said something in the faint, remote voice of the sleep-talker. Heather could not hear what he said, but she thought at once of last night; she had been nearly asleep, curled up next to him, when he had said something aloud: air per annum, it sounded like. "What?" she had said, and he had said nothing, he was asleep. As he was now.

Her heart contracted within her as she watched him lying there, his hands quiet at his sides, vulnerable.

Haber had risen, and now pressed a white button on the side of the machine at the head of the couch; some of the electrode wires went to it, and some to the EEG machine, which she recognized. The thing in the wall must be the Augmentor, the thing all the research was about.

Haber came over to her, where she sat sunk deep in a huge leather armchair. Real leather, she had forgotten what real leather felt like. It was like the vinyleathers, but more interesting to the fingers. She was frightened. She did not understand what was going on. She looked up askance at the big man standing before her, the bear-shaman-god.

"This is the culmination, Mrs. Orr," he was saying in a lowered voice, "of a long series of suggested dreams. We've been building toward this session—this dream—for weeks now. I'm glad you came, I didn't think to ask you, but your presence is an added boon in making him feel completely secure and trustful. He knows I can't pull any tricks with you around! Right? Actually I'm pretty confident of success. It'll do the trick. The dependency on sleeping drugs will be quite broken, once the obsessive fear of dreaming is erased. It's purely a matter of conditioning. . . . I've got to keep an eye on that EEG, he'll be dreaming now." Quick and massive, he moved across the room. She sat still, watching George's calm face, from which the expression of concentration, all expression, was gone. So he might look in death.

Dr. Haber was busy with his machines, restlessly busy, bowing over them, adjusting them, watching them. He paid no heed at all to George.

"There," he said softly—not to her, Heather thought; he was his own audience. "That's it. Now. Now a little break, second-stage sleep for a bit, between dreams." He did something to the equipment in the wall. "Then we'll run a little test. . . ." He came over to her again; she wished

157

he would really ignore her instead of pretending to talk to her. He seemed not to know the uses of silence. "Your husband has been of inestimable service to our research here, Mrs. Orr. A unique patient. What we've learned about the nature of dreaming, and the employment of dreams in both positive and negative conditioning therapy, will be of literally inestimable value in every walk of life. You know what HURAD stands for. Human Utility: Research and Development. Well, what we've learned from this case will be of immense, literally immense, human utility. An amazing thing to develop out of what appeared to be a routine case of minor drug abuse! The most amazing thing about it is that the hacks down at the Med School had the wits to notice anything special in the case and refer it up to me. You seldom get so much acuteness in academic clinical psychologists." His eye had been on his watch all along, and he now said, "Well, back to Baby," and swiftly recrossed the room. He diddled with the Augmentor thing again and said aloud, "George. You're still asleep, but you can hear me. You can hear and understand me perfectly. Nod a little if you hear me."

The calm face did not change, but the head nodded once. Like the head of a puppet on a string.

"Good. Now, listen carefully. You're going to have another vivid dream. You'll dream that . . . that there's a mural photograph on the wall, here in my office. A big picture of Mount Hood, all covered with snow. You'll dream that you see the mural there on the wall behind the desk, right here in my office. All right. Now you're going to sleep, and dream. . . . Antwerp."

He bustled and bowed at his machinery again. "There," he whispered under his breath. "There . . . O.K. . . . right."

The machines were still. George lay still. Even Haber ceased to move and mutter. There was no sound in the big, softly lit room, with its wall of glass looking out into the rain. Haber stood by the EEG, his head turned to the wall behind the desk.

Nothing happened.

Heather moved the fingers of her left hand in a tiny circle on the resilient, grainy surface of the armchair, the stuff that had once been the skin of a living animal, the intermediate surface between a cow and the universe. The tune of the old record they had played yesterday came into her head and wouldn't get out again.

What do you see when you turn out the light?
I can't tell you, but I know it's mine. . . .

She wouldn't have thought that Haber could hold still, keep silent, for so long. Only once, his fingers flicked out to a dial. Then he stood immobile again, watching the blank wall.

George sighed, raised a hand sleepily, relaxed again, and woke. He blinked and sat up. His eyes went at once to Heather, as if to make sure she was there.

Haber frowned, and with a jumpy, startled movement pushed the lower button of the Augmentor. "What the hell!" he said. He stared at the EEG screen, still jigging with lively little traces. "The Augmentor was feeding you d-state patterns, how the hell did you wake up?"

"I don't know." George yawned. "I just did. Didn't you instruct me to wake soon?"

"I generally do. On the signal. But how the hell did you override the pattern stimulation from the Augmentor. . . . I'll have to increase the power; obviously been going at this too tentatively." He was now talking to the Augmentor itself, there was no doubt of it. When that conversation was done he turned abruptly on George and said, "All right. What was the dream?"

"Dreamed there was a picture of Mount Hood on the wall there, behind my wife."

Haber's eyes flicked to the bare redwood-paneled wall, and back to George.

"Anything else? An earlier dream—any recall of it?"

"I think so. Wait a minute. . . . I guess I dreamed that I was dreaming, or something. It was confused. I was in a store. That's it—I was in Meier and Frank's buying a new suit, it had to have a blue tunic, because I was going to have a new job, or something. I can't remember. But anyhow, they had a guide sheet that told you what you

159

ought to weigh if you're so tall, and vice versa. And I was right in the middle of both the height scale and the weight scale for average-build men."

"Normal, in other words," Haber said, and suddenly laughed. He had a huge laugh. It startled Heather badly, after the tension and the silence.

"That's fine, George. That's just fine." He clapped George on the shoulder, and began taking the electrodes off his head. "We have made it. We have arrived. You're in the clear! Do you know it?"

"I believe so," George replied mildly.

"The big load's off your shoulders. Right?"

"And onto yours?"

"And onto mine. Right!" Again the big, gusty laugh, a little overprolonged. Heather wondered if Haber was always like this, or was in a state of extreme excitement.

"Dr. Haber," her husband said, "have you ever talked to an Alien about dreaming?"

"An Aldebaranian, you mean? No. Forde in Washington tried out a couple of our tests on some of 'em, along with a whole series of psychological tests, but the results were meaningless. We simply haven't licked the communications problem there. They're intelligent but Irchevsky, our best xenobiologist, thinks they may not be rational at all, and that what looks like socially integrative behavior among humans is nothing but a kind of instinctual adaptive mimicry. No telling for sure. Can't get an EEG on 'em and as a matter of fact we can't even find out whether they sleep or not, let alone dream!"

"Do you know the term *iahklu'*?"

Haber paused momentarily. "Heard it. It's untranslatable. You've decided it means 'dream,' eh?"

George shook his head. "I don't know what it means. I don't pretend to have any knowledge you haven't got, but I do think that before you go on with the, with the application of the new technique, Dr. Haber, before you dream, you ought to talk with one of the Aliens."

"Which one?" The flick of irony was clear.

"Any one. It doesn't matter."

Haber laughed. "Talk about what, George?"

160

Heather saw her husband's light eyes flash as he looked up at the bigger man. "About me. About dreaming. About *iahklu'*. It doesn't matter. So long as you *listen*. They'll know what you're getting at, they're a lot more experienced than we are at all this."

"At what?"

"At dreaming—at what dreaming is an aspect of. They've done it for a long time. For always, I guess. They are of the dream time. I don't understand it, I can't say it in words. Everything dreams. The play of form, of being, is the dreaming of substance. Rocks have their dreams, and the earth changes. . . . But when the mind becomes conscious, when the rate of evolution speeds up, then you have to be careful. Careful of the world. You must learn the way. You must learn the skills, the art, the limits. A conscious mind must be part of the whole, intentionally and carefully—as the rock is part of the whole unconsciously. Do you see? Does it mean anything to you?"

"It's not new to me, if that's what you mean. World soul and so on. Prescientific synthesis. Mysticism is one approach to the nature of dreaming, or of reality, though it's not acceptable to those willing to use reason, and able to."

"I don't know if that's true," George said without the least resentment, though he was very earnest. "But just out of scientific curiosity, then, at least try this: before testing the Augmentor on yourself, before you turn it on, when you're starting your autosuggestion, say this: *Er' perrehnne.* Aloud or in your mind. Once. Clearly. Try it."

"Why?"

"Because it works."

" 'Works' how?"

"You get a little help from your friends," George said. He stood up. Heather stared at him in terror. What he had been saying sounded crazy—Haber's cure had driven him insane, she had known it would. But Haber was not responding—was he?—as he would to incoherent or psychotic talk.

"*Iahklu'* is too much for one person to handle alone," George was saying, "it gets out of hand. They know what's

161

involved in controlling it. Or, not exactly controlling it, that's not the right word; but keeping it where it belongs, going the right way. . . . I don't understand it. Maybe you will. Ask their help. Say *Er' perrehnne* before you . . . before you press the ON button."

"You may have something there," Haber said. "Might be worth investigating. I'll get onto it, George. I'll have one of the Aldebaranians from the Culture Center up and see if I can get some information on this. . . . All Greek to you, eh, Mrs. Orr? This husband of yours should have gone into the shrink game, the research end of it; he's wasted as a draftsman." Why did he say that? George was a parks-and-playgrounds designer. "He's got the flair, he's a natural. Never thought of hooking the Aldebaranians in on this, but he might just have a real idea there. But maybe you're just as glad he's not a shrink, eh? Awful to have your spouse analyzing your unconscious desires across the dinner table, eh?" He boomed and thundered, showing them out. Heather was bewildered, nearly in tears.

"I hate him," she said fiercely, on the descending spiral of the escalator. "He's a horrible man. False. A big fake!"

George took her arm. He said nothing.

"Are you through? Really through? You won't need drugs any more, and you're all through these awful sessions?"

"I think so. He'll file my papers, and in six weeks I should get a notice of clearance. If I behave myself." He smiled, a little tiredly. "This was tough on you, but honey, but it wasn't on me. Not this time. I'm hungry, though. Where'll we go for dinner? The Casa Boliviana?"

"Chinatown," she said, and then caught herself. "Ha-ha," she added. The old Chinese district had been cleared away along with the rest of downtown, at least ten years ago. For some reason she had completely forgotten that for a moment. "I mean Ruby Loo's," she said, confused.

George held her arm a little closer. "Fine," he said.

It was easy to get to; the funicular line stopped across the river in the old Lloyd Center, once the biggest shopping center in the world, back before the Crash. Nowadays the vast multilevel parking lots were gone along with the dinosaurs, and many of the shops and stores along the two-level mall were empty, boarded up. The ice rink had not been filled in twenty years. No water ran in the bizarre, romantic fountains of twisted metal. Small ornamental trees had grown up towering; their roots cracked the walkways for yards around their cylindrical planters. Voices and footsteps rang overclearly, a little hollowly, before and behind one, walking those long, half-lit, half-derelict arcades.

Ruby Loo's was on the upper level. The branches of a horse chestnut almost hid the glass façade. Overhead, the sky was an intense delicate green, that color seen briefly on spring evenings when there is a clearing after rain. Heather looked up into that jade heaven, remote, improbable, serene; her heart lifted, she felt anxiety begin to slip off her like a shed skin. But it did not last. There was a curious reversal, a shifting. Something seemed to catch at her, to hold her. She almost stopped walking, and looked down from the sky of jade into the empty, heavy-shadowed walks before her. This was a strange place. "It's spooky up here," she said.

George shrugged; but his face looked tense and rather grim.

A wind had come up, too warm for the Aprils of the old days, a wet, hot wind moving the great green-fingered branches of the chestnut, stirring litter far down the long, deserted turnings. The red neon sign behind the moving branches seemed to dim and waver with the wind, to change shape; it didn't say Ruby Loo's, it didn't say anything any more. Nothing said anything. Nothing had meaning. The wind blew hollow in the hollow courts. Heather turned away from George and went off toward the nearest wall; she was in tears. In pain her instinct was to hide, to get in a corner of a wall and hide.

"What is it, honey. . . . It's all right. Hang on, it'll be all right."

I am going insane, she thought; it wasn't George, it wasn't George all along, it was me.

"It'll be all right," he whispered once more, but she

163

heard in his voice that he did not believe it. She felt in his hands that he did not believe it.

"What's wrong," she cried despairing. "What's wrong?"

"I don't know," he said, almost inattentively. He had lifted his head and turned a little from her, though he still held her to him to stop her crying fit. He seemed to be watching, to be listening. She felt the heart beat hard and steady in his chest.

"Heather, listen. I'm going to have to go back."

"Go back where? What is it that's wrong?" Her voice was thin and high.

"To Haber. I have to go. Now. Wait for me—in the restaurant. Wait for me, Heather. Don't follow me." He was off. She had to follow. He went, not looking back, fast, down the long stairs, under the arcades, past the dry fountains, out to the funicular station. A car was waiting, there at the end of the line; he hopped in. She scrambled on, her breath hurting in her chest, just as the car began to pull out. "What the *hell,* George!"

"I'm sorry." He was panting, too. "I have to get there. I didn't want to take you into it."

"Into what?" She detested him. They sat on facing seats, puffing at each other. "What is this crazy performance? What are you going back there for?"

"Haber is—" George's voice went dry for a moment. "He is dreaming," he said. A deep mindless terror crawled inside Heather; she ignored it.

"Dreaming what? So what?"

"Look out the window."

She had looked only at him, while they ran and since they had got onto the car. The funicular was crossing the river now, high above the water. But there was no water. The river had run dry. The bed of it lay cracked and oozing in the lights of the bridges, foul, full of grease and bones and lost tools and dying fish. The great ships lay careened and ruined by the towering, slimy docks.

The buildings of downtown Portland, the Capital of the World, the high, new, handsome cubes of stone and glass interspersed with measured doses of green, the fortresses of Government—Research and Development, Communications, Industry, Economic Planning, Environmental Control—were melting. They were getting soggy and shaky, like jello left out in the sun. The corners had already run down the sides, leaving great creamy smears.

The funicular was going very fast and not stopping at stations: something must be wrong with the cable, Heather thought without personal involvement. They swung rapidly over the dissolving city, low enough to hear the rumbling and the cries.

As the car ran up higher, Mount Hood came into view, behind George's head as he sat facing her. He saw the lurid light reflected on her face or in her eyes, perhaps, for he turned at once to look, to see the vast inverted cone of fire.

The car swung wild in the abyss, between the unforming city and the formless sky.

"Nothing seems to go quite right today," said a woman farther back in the car, in a loud, quivering voice.

The light of the eruption was terrible and gorgeous. Its huge, material, geological vigor was reassuring, compared to the hollow area that now lay ahead of the car, at the upper end of the line.

The presentiment which had seized Heather as she looked down from the jade sky was now a presence. It was there. It was an area, or perhaps a time-period, of a sort of emptiness. It was the presence of absence: an unquantifiable entity without qualities, into which all things fell and from which nothing came forth. It was horrible, and it was nothing. It was the wrong way.

Into this, as the funicular car stopped at its terminus, George went. He looked back at her as he went, crying out, "Wait for me, Heather! Don't follow me, don't come!"

But though she tried to obey him, it came to her. It was growing out from the center rapidly. She found that all things were gone and that she was lost in the panic dark, crying out her husband's name with no voice, desolate, until she sank down in a ball curled about the center of her own being, and fell forever through the dry abyss.

By the power of will, which is indeed great when

165

exercised in the right way at the right time, George Orr found beneath his feet the hard marble of the steps up to the HURAD Tower. He walked forward, while his eyes informed him that he walked on mist, on mud, on decayed corpses, on innumerable tiny toads. It was very cold, yet there was a smell of hot metal and burning hair or flesh. He crossed the lobby; gold letters from the aphorism around the dome leapt about him momentarily, MAN MANKIND M N A A A. The A's tried to trip his feet. He stepped onto a moving walkway though it was not visible to him; he stepped onto the helical escalator and rode it up into nothing, supporting it continually by the firmness of his will. He did not even shut his eyes.

Up on the top story, the floor was ice. It was about a finger's width thick, and quite clear. Through it could be seen the stars of the Southern Hemisphere. Orr stepped out onto it and all the stars rang loud and false, like cracked bells. The foul smell was much worse, making him gag. He went forward, holding out his hand. The panel of the door of Haber's outer office was there to meet it; he could not see it but he touched it. A wolf howled. The lava moved toward the city.

He went on and came to the last door. He pushed it open. On the other side of it there was nothing.

"Help me," he said aloud, for the void drew him, pulled at him. He had not the strength all by himself to get through nothingness and out the other side.

There was a sort of dull rousing in his mind; he thought of Tiua'k Ennbe Ennbe, and of the bust of Schubert, and of Heather's voice saying furiously, "What the *hell*, George!" This seemed to be all he had to cross nothingness on. He went forward. He knew as he went that he would lose all he had.

He entered the eye of the nightmare.

It was a cold, vaguely moving, rotating darkness made of fear, that pulled him aside, pulled him apart. He knew where the Augmentor stood. He put out his mortal hand along the way things go. He touched it; felt for the lower button, and pushed it once.

He crouched down then, covering his eyes and cowering,

for the fear had taken his mind. When he raised his head and looked, the world re-existed. It was not in good condition, but it was there.

They weren't in the HURAD Tower, but in some dingier, commoner office which he had never seen before. Haber lay sprawled on the couch, massive, his beard jutting up. Red-brown beard again, whitish skin, no longer gray. The eyes were half open and saw nothing.

Orr pulled away the electrodes whose wires ran like threadworms between Haber's skull and the Augmentor. He looked at the machine, its cabinets all standing open; it should be destroyed, he thought. But he had no idea how to do it, nor any will to try. Destruction was not his line; and a machine is more blameless, more sinless even than any animal. It has no intentions whatsoever but our own.

"Dr. Haber," he said, shaking the big, heavy shoulders a little. "Haber! Wake up!"

After a while the big body moved, and presently sat up. It was all slack and loose. The massive, handsome head hung between the shoulders. The mouth was loose. The eyes looked straight forward into the dark, into the void, into the unbeing at the center of William Haber; they were no longer opaque, they were empty.

Orr became afraid of him physically, and backed away from him.

I've got to get help, he thought, I can't handle this alone. . . . He left the office, went out through an unfamiliar waiting room, ran down the stairs. He had never been in this building and had no idea what it was, or where. When he came out into the street, he knew that it was a Portland street, but that was all. It was nowhere near Washington Park, or the west hills. It was no street he had ever walked on.

The emptiness of Haber's being, the effective nightmare, radiating outward from the dreaming brain, had undone connections. The continuity which had always held between the worlds or timelines of Orr's dreaming had now been broken. Chaos had entered in. He had few and incoherent memories of this existence he was now in;

167

almost all he knew came from the other memories, the other dreamtimes.

Other people, less aware than he, might be better equipped for this shift of existence: but they would be more frightened by it, having no explanation. They would be finding the world radically, senselessly, suddenly changed, with no possible rational cause of change. There would be much death and terror following Dr. Haber's dream.

And loss. And loss.

He knew he had lost her; had known it since he stepped out, with her help, into the panic void surrounding the dreamer. She was lost along with the world of the gray people and the huge, fake building into which he had run, leaving her alone in the ruin and dissolution of the nightmare. She was gone.

He did not try to get help for Haber. There was no help for Haber. Nor for himself. He had done all he would ever do. He walked on along the distracted streets. He saw from streetsigns that he was in the northeast part of Portland, an area he had never known much of. The houses were low, and at corners there was sometimes a view of the mountain. He saw that the eruption had ceased; had never, in fact, begun. Mount Hood rose dun-violet into the darkening April sky, dormant. The mountain slept.

Dreaming, dreaming.

Orr walked without goal, following one street and then another; he was exhausted, so that he sometimes wanted to lie down there on the pavement and rest for a while, yet he kept going. He was approaching a business section now, coming closer to the river. The city, half wrecked and half transformed, a jumble and mess of grandiose plans and incomplete memories, swarmed like Bedlam; fires and insanities ran from house to house. And yet people went about their business as always: there were two men looting a jewelry shop, and past them came a woman who held her bawling, red-faced baby in her arms and walked purposefully home.

Wherever home was.

11

Starlight asked Non-Entity, 'Master, do you exist? or do you not exist?' He got no answer to his question, however. . . .

—Chuang Tse: XXII

Some time that night, as Orr was trying to find his way through the suburbs of chaos to Corbett Avenue, an Aldebaranian Alien stopped him and persuaded him to come with it. He came along, docile. He asked it after a while if it was Tiua'k Ennbe Ennbe, but he did not ask with much conviction, and did not seem to mind when the Alien explained, rather laboriously, that he was called Jor Jor and it was called E'nememen Asfah.

It took him to its apartment near the river, over a bicycle repair shop and next door to the Hope Eternal Gospel Mission, which was pretty full up, tonight. All over the world the various gods were being requested, more or less politely, for an explanation of what had occurred between 6:25 and 7:08 P.M. Pacific Standard Time. Sweetly discordant, "Rock of Ages" rang underfoot as they climbed dark stairs to a second-story flat. The Alien there suggested that he lie down on the bed, as he looked tired. "Sleep that knits up the ravell'd sleave of care," it said.

"To sleep, perchance to dream; aye, there's the rub," Orr replied. There was, he thought, something to the curious manner in which the Aliens communicated; but he was much too tired to decide what. "Where will you sleep?" he inquired, sitting down heavily on the bed.

169

"No where," the Alien replied, its toneless voice dividing the word into two equally significant wholes.

Orr stooped to unlace his shoes. He didn't want to get the Alien's bedspread dirty with his shoes, that would be scarcely a fair return for kindness. Stooping made him dizzy. "I am tired," he said. "I did a lot today. That is, I did something. The only thing I have ever done. I pressed a button. It took the entire will power, the accumulated strength of my entire existence, to press one damned OFF button."

"You have lived well," the Alien said.

It was standing in a corner, apparently intending to stand there indefinitely.

It was not standing there, Orr thought: not in the same way that he would stand, or sit, or lie, or be. It was standing there in the way that he, in a dream, might be standing. It was there in the sense that in a dream one is somewhere.

He lay back. He clearly sensed the pity and protective compassion of the Alien standing across the dark room. It saw him, not with eyes, as short-lived, fleshly, armorless, a strange creature, infinitely vulnerable, adrift in the gulfs of the possible: something that needed help. He didn't mind. He did need help. Weariness took him over, picked him up like a current of the sea into which he was sinking slowly. *"Er' perrehnne,"* he muttered, surrendering to sleep.

"Er' perrehnne," replied E'nememen Asfah, soundlessly.

Orr slept. He dreamed. There was no rub. His dreams, like waves of the deep sea far from any shore, came and went, rose and fell, profound and harmless, breaking nowhere, changing nothing. They danced the dance among all the other waves in the sea of being. Through his sleep the great, green sea turtles dived, swimming with heavy inexhaustible grace through the depths, in their element.

In early June the trees were in full leaf and the roses blooming. All over the city the large, old-fashioned ones, tough as weeds, called the Portland Rose, flowered pink on thorny stems. Things had settled down pretty well. The economy was recovering. People were mowing their lawns.

Orr was at the Federal Asylum for the Insane at Linnton, a little north of Portland. The buildings, put up early in the nineties, stood on a great bluff overlooking the water meadows of the Willamette and the Gothic elegance of the St. Johns Bridge. They had been horribly overcrowded there in late April and May, with the plague of mental breakdowns that had followed on the inexplicable events of the evening that was now referred to as "The Break"; but that had eased off, and asylum routine was back to its understaffed, overcrowded, terrible norm.

A tall, soft-spoken orderly took Orr upstairs to the single-bed rooms in the north wing. The door leading into this wing and the doors of all the rooms in it were heavy, with a little spyhole grating five feet up, and all of them were locked.

"It's not that he's troublesome," the orderly said as he unlocked the corridor door. "Never been violent. But he had this bad effect on the others. We tried him in two wards. No go. The others were scared of him, never saw anything like it. They all affect each other and get panics and wild nights and so on, but not like this. They were scared of *him*. Be clawing at the doors, nights, to get away from him. And all he ever did was just lay there. Well, you see everything here, sooner or later. He don't care where he is, I guess. Here you are." He unlocked the door and preceded Orr into the room. "Visitor, Dr. Haber," he said.

Haber was thin. The blue and white pajamas hung lank on him. His hair and beard were cut shorter, but were well cared for and neat. He sat on the bed and stared at the void.

"Dr. Haber," Orr said, but his voice failed; he felt excruciating pity, and fear. He knew what Haber was looking at. He had seen it himself. He was looking at the world after April 1998. He was looking at the world as misunderstood by the mind: the bad dream.

There is a bird in a poem by T. S. Eliot who says that mankind cannot bear very much reality; but the bird is mistaken. A man can endure the entire weight of the universe for eighty years. It is unreality that he cannot bear.

Haber was lost. He had lost touch.

Orr tried to speak again, but found no words. He backed out, and the orderly, right with him, closed and locked the door.

"I can't," Orr said. "There's no way."

"No way," the orderly said.

Going down the corridor, he added in his soft voice, "Dr. Walters tells me he was a very promising scientist."

Orr returned to downtown Portland by boat. Transportation was still rather confused; pieces, remnants, and commencements of about six different public-transportation systems cluttered up the city. Reed College had a subway station, but no subway; the funicular to Washington Park ended at the entrance to a tunnel which went halfway under the Willamette and then stopped. Meanwhile, an enterprising fellow had refitted a couple of boats that used to run tours up and down the Willamette and Columbia, and was using them as ferries on regular runs between Linnton, Vancouver, Portland, and Oregon City. It made a pleasant trip.

Orr had taken a long lunch hour for the visit to the asylum. His employer, the Alien E'nememen Asfah, was indifferent to hours worked and interested only in work done. When one did it was one's own concern. Orr did a good deal of his in his head, lying in bed half-awake for an hour before he got up in the morning.

It was three o'clock when he got back to the Kitchen Sink and sat down in front of his drafting table in the workshop. Asfah was in the showroom waiting on customers. He had a staff of three designers, and contracts with various manufacturers who made kitchen equipment of all sorts, bowls, cookware, implements, tools, everything short of heavy appliances. Industry and distribution had been left in disastrous confusion by The Break; national and international government had been so distraught for weeks that a state of laissez faire had prevailed perforce, and small private firms that had been able to keep going or get started during this period were in a good position. In Oregon a number of these firms, all handling material goods of one kind or another, were run by

172

Aldebaranians; they were good managers and extraordinary salesmen, though they had to hire human beings for all handwork. The Government liked them because they willingly accepted governmental constraints and controls, for the world economy was gradually pulling itself back together. People were even talking about the Gross National Product again, and President Merdle had predicted a return to normalcy by Christmas.

Asfah sold retail as well as wholesale, and the Kitchen Sink was popular for its sturdy wares and fair prices. Since The Break, housewives, refurnishing the unexpected kitchens they had found themselves cooking in that evening in April, had come in increasing numbers. Orr was looking over some wood samples for cutting boards when he heard one saying, "I'd like one of those egg whisks," and because the voice reminded him of his wife's voice he got up and looked into the showroom. Asfah was showing something to a middle-sized brown woman of thirty or so, with short, black, wiry hair on a well-shaped head.

"Heather," he said, coming forward.

She turned. She looked at him for what seemed a long time. "Orr," she said. "George Orr. Right? When did I know you?"

"In—" He hesitated. "Aren't you a lawyer?"

E'nememen Asfah stood immense in greenish armor, holding an egg whisk.

"Nope. Legal secretary. I work for Rutti and Goodhue, in the Pendleton Building."

"That must be it. I was in there once. Do you, do you like that? I designed it." He took another egg whisk from the bin and displayed it to her. "Good balance, see. And it works fast. They usually make the wires too taut, or too heavy, except in France."

"It's good-looking," she said. "I have an old electric mixer but I wanted at least to hang that on the wall. You work here? You didn't use to. I remember now. You were in some office on Stark Street, and you were seeing a doctor on Voluntary Therapy."

He had no idea what, or how much, she recalled, nor how to fit it in with his own multiple memories.

His wife, of course, had been gray-skinned. There were still gray people now, it was said, particularly in the Middle West and Germany, but most of the rest had gone back to white, brown, black, red, yellow, and mixtures. His wife had been a gray person, a far gentler person than this one, he thought. This Heather carried a big black handbag with a brass snap, and probably a half pint of brandy inside; she came on hard. His wife had been unaggressive and, though courageous, timid in manner. This was not his wife, but a fiercer woman, vivid and difficult.

"That's right," he said. "Before The Break. We had . . . Actually, Miss Lelache, we had a date for lunch. At Dave's, on Ankeny. We never made it."

"I'm not Miss Lelache, that's my maiden name. I'm Mrs. Andrews."

She eyed him with curiosity. He stood and endured reality.

"My husband was killed in the war in the Near East," she added.

"Yes," Orr said.

"Do you design all these things?"

"Most of the tools and stuff. And the cookware. Look, do you like this?" He hauled out a copper-bottom tea-kettle, massive and yet elegant, as proportioned by necessity as a sailing ship.

"Who wouldn't?" she said, putting out her hands. He gave it to her. She hefted and admired it. "I like things," she said.

He nodded.

"You're a real artist. It's beautiful."

"Mr. Orr is expert with tangibles," the proprietor put in, toneless, speaking from the left elbow.

"Listen, I remember," Heather said suddenly. "Of course, it was before The Break, that's why it's all mixed up in my mind. You dreamed, I mean, you thought you dreamed things that came true. Didn't you? And the doctor was making you do more and more of it, and you didn't want him to, and you were looking for a way to get out of Voluntary Therapy with him without getting clobbered with Obligatory. See, I do remember it. Did you ever get assigned to another shrink?"

"No. Outgrew 'em," Orr said, and laughed. She also laughed.

"What did you do about the dreams?"

"Oh . . . went on dreaming."

"I thought you could change the world. Is this the best you could do for us—this mess?"

"It'll have to do," he said.

He would have preferred less of a mess himself, but it wasn't up to him. And at least it had her in it. He had sought her as best he could, had not found her, and had turned to his work for solace; it had not given much, but it was the work he was fit to do, and he was a patient man. But now his dry and silent grieving for his lost wife must end, for there she stood, the fierce, recalcitrant, and fragile stranger, forever to be won again.

He knew her, he knew his stranger, how to keep her talking and how to make her laugh. He said finally, "Would you like a cup of coffee? There's a café next door. It's time for my break."

"The hell it is," she said; it was quarter to five. She glanced over at the Alien. "Sure I'd like some coffee, but—"

"I'll be back in ten minutes. E'nememen Asfah," Orr said to his employer as he went for his raincoat.

"Take evening," the Alien said. "There is time. There are returns. To go is to return."

"Thank you very much," Orr said, and shook hands with his boss. The big green flipper was cool on his human hand. He went out with Heather into the warm, rainy afternoon of summer. The Alien watched them from within the glass-fronted shop, as a sea creature might watch from an aquarium, seeing them pass and disappear into the mist.

AVON ⬢ MEANS THE BEST
IN SCIENCE FICTION!